Owing to a drugs war, a man on a walking holiday is forced to share his bed with a complete stranger; following his wife's death, a man discovers she has made bizarre plans for his future; a woman decides to clear her clutter, with unforeseen consequences; a young lad eats a slice of forbidden cake and wishes he hadn't; and a young woman takes part in an army pie-eating contest.

These and thirty-five other hilarious stories by Simon J. Wood, a master of the 'flash fiction' format, are guaranteed to generate laughs on the Richter scale!

To Heather
with best wishes

Simon J. Wood
x

Letters from Reuben and Other Stories

Also by Simon J. Wood:

Bound in Morocco: A Short Story of Intrigue

To Cut a Short Story Short: 111 Little Stories

To Cut a Short Story Short, vol. II: 88 Little Stories

The Window Crack'd and Other Stories: 40 Little Tales of Horror and the Supranatural

Flash Friction: To Cut a Short Story Short, vol. III: 72 Little Stories

Letters from Reuben and Other Stories

40 Little Tales of Mirth

Simon J. Wood

Copyright © 2021 by Simon J. Wood

All rights reserved. This book or parts thereof may not be reproduced in any form, stored in any retrieval system, or transmitted in any form by any means – electronic, mechanical, photocopy, recording, or otherwise – without prior written permission of the publisher, except as provided by international copyright law. For permission requests, please contact the author via the website below.

This is a work of fiction. Any resemblance to actual persons, living or dead, is entirely coincidental.

Visit the author's website at:

https://simonjwood.wordpress.com/

Letters from Reuben/Simon J. Wood – 1st Edition.

For Nancy, with gratitude.

Preface

Following on from *To Cut a Short Story Short, volumes I* and *II* I am pleased to present another volume of 'flash fiction,' this time, curated stories of humour in various shades.

The stories range from 150 words to 2200 words and are around 850 words on average. For the curious – and/or flash fiction *aficionado* – the word count of each story is given in the appendix.

I sincerely hope that these stories will bring you pleasure and, for a little while, rescue you from the gloom and doom that seem to surround us daily! If so, a positive review on Amazon would be much appreciated.

Colonel: "Watkins, why did you join the army?"

Watkins: "For the water-skiing and the travel, sir. Not for the killing, sir. I asked them to put it on my form, sir: *'no* killing'."

Colonel: "Watkins, are you a pacifist?"

Watkins: "No, sir. I'm not a pacifist, sir. I'm a coward."

— *'Monty Python's Flying Circus'*

Contents

Contact 1

Dinner with the Colonel 4

The Listening... 7

Danny and the Dolly Bird 10

Tranquil Beginnings 14

Never Lovelier... 17

The Magic Roundabout 20

When the Fat Man Croaks... 22

All Apologies (A Writers' A-Z) 25

Animal Magic.. 34

Pie in the Sky... 37

What's in a Name? 40

Shelly in the Jungle 42

Something to Do With the Sea 45

Wounded Walking... 48

Tastes Like Hippopotamus to Me 51

Here's Looking at Your Kid.. 54

Stone the Crows 57

The Name is Grey.. 60

The Old Fuse Trick.. 62

There Was None Bolder 65

Letters from Reuben.. 68

Free Money.. 70

In Memoriam 73

Postcard from Hispaniola 76

Just One Little Crumb	77
The Ballad of Johnny Fang	82
The Boy in the Attic	84
Behind Locked Doors	87
Martian Holiday	90
Dog Story	94
The Bride	97
The Invisible Man	100
A Brush with Teeth	103
Memory Lane	106
As Safe as S*it	110
A Question of Semantics	113
The Price of Silver	116
Gender Concerns	119
Goodbye Bernie, Hello Samantha	122
Appendix – Word Count of Stories	126

Contact

The day my life changed was the day the lives of everyone changed. Finally, there was irrefutable, cast-iron evidence of extra-terrestrial civilisation. Evidence that couldn't be fobbed off by governments as weather balloons, Venus, hallucination or just being plain drunk. But for me it was different. There I'd been, watching the whole shebang from my weightless viewpoint, floating around the International Space Station or ISS.

"Hey, Jabez, there it is. I've got it on the viewing screen!" astronaut Vladimir Chekhov exclaimed.

"Wow. Let's have a look." There, on our wall-to-wall cinema was a tiny pinprick of light, still tens of thousands of miles away but, without doubt, on its way to good 'ol Planet Earth.

Since first detected by Pan-STARRS, a specially designed telescope to monitor the cosmos for unidentified movement of heavenly – and not-so-heavenly – bodies, the approaching object had been dismissed as a comet or asteroid, never mind the fact that at Jupiter it had accelerated at a rate faster than gravity predicted. Astrophysicists, that lofty breed of super intelligent humans – or so they thought – had said it was down to 'outgassing' of some unknown – and invisible – substance, thus accelerating the object by 'natural' means.

But as it grew closer, instruments could no longer refute that it was some kind of 'light-sail' craft.

"Hey, dad, what's with this spacecraft coming to earth?"

I'd looked at Richardson's earnest young face. Since his mother had died, our weekly meetings via the ISS video interface had been all we'd had to look forward to. All the technology in the world couldn't replace a pretty face, bright blue eyes, wide smile, and the tight hug of a beautiful woman. But, like they say, 'Life moves on.' "Well, telescopes the world over have seen this thing. And no one can say it isn't real now."

"What is it though, dad, do you think it might be dangerous, a weapon or something?"

I looked out of the window, down onto our brilliant blue marble in the endless blackness of space and sighed. "Hey, Rich, you've been watching too much science fiction. They're likely just like you and me. They just wanna say 'hello'." I kept to myself how I'd lain awake at night worrying about this being some kind of doomsday device, designed to decimate our planet, if not destroy it like you'd burst a beautiful sparkling bubble. One minute, swirling rainbow colour, the next a pop ... and empty space.

But as the object grew closer it seemed like there was no 'they,' not alive, anyway. There was no signal of any description, just the brightness and a spinning motion and silence.

"Jabez, I don't want you to go, honey."

I could see a film of moisture on Hannah's eyes. "Look, sweetheart, this is the greatest opportunity I, or anyone in my family's had, like, ever. Just think, the ISS, practically the most advanced bit of machinery ever made, and I'll be onboard! It's only for a year and you and Richardson can call me every week. We can see each other on the big screen. It's like we'll be in the same room."

Hannah had smiled wistfully, "Well, not quite, we won't be able to hug and, well, y'know." She blushed. "Do it."

I'd laughed. "Don't worry sweetheart, I'll make up for it when I get back! And time passes quickly."

But no matter how quickly time passes, it can't bring someone back from a fatal auto accident, nor heal the hurt left by the huge empty space inside, greater even than the infinite universe outside.

Now, from our exalted places on the roof of the world, we were privy to the latest developments from NASA. It had indeed been a light sail craft, and by man's, or that is to say, NASA's, ingenuity, a rocket had been modified in time to launch into space and capture the alien craft. One week earlier it had returned to earth, since when there'd been no news, other than NASA's announcement that, 'This appears to be an alien craft propelled by a light sail that has been sailing across the universe for an indeterminate time, possibly millions or even billions of years. It is currently undergoing investigative procedures." That was it, to the chagrin of the whole, impatient world.

But now the communicator buzzed. The serious face of NASA's William Bark appeared on the screen. "Hiya, Jabez, well we've got some intel on the aliens, it's not good."

I felt myself breaking out in a cold sweat. "It's not a weapon, is it?"

Bark waved a hand away. "Nope, nothing like that. The sail itself is pretty similar to sails we've developed here on earth, nothing new material-wise."

"That's disappointing."

"Yeah, there's nothing electronic either. Seems it was likely blasted through space by the impetus of a high-powered laser, maybe half the speed of light, originally."

I felt impatient. "Well, what is it then?"

Bark sighed. "Look, we're not sure what to announce, right now. There's a cylinder full of empty containers, plastics, metals, but nothing new to science, and a lot of organic substance."

"Organic substance?"

"Yeah, well, it looks like these aliens blasted their rubbish into space, saving on landfill, I guess. So, what we've got is a load of rubbish, literally."

"But what about the organic stuff?"

"Well, seems they didn't want to overload their sewage plants either. Would you believe … billion-year-old shit?"

Dinner with the Colonel

Moorland, cattle grids and small cottages, built from blocks of grey-green stone; that was Clay Hill. Sue and I had moved there three months earlier. The folks seemed friendly enough, but there was an odd reserve in them that was difficult to put your finger on. Despite now living in one of the more picturesque areas of Britain, life seemed rather dull.

I was sitting at my desk, gazing out through the window and over the purple heather to the brown hills beyond. Above them, clouds ambled by, high wispy cirrus in no hurry to go anywhere and cumulonimbus, resembling floating towers of shaving foam. The door opened and Sue came in, carrying a basket of eggs. She pecked me on the cheek, put the eggs on a worn oak table and plumped herself down in an old armchair. "Well, I just had an interesting chat with Mavis in the shop."

"Oh."

"Yes, she said she was surprised not to have seen us at the service on Sunday."

"Why? We're not religious."

"Yes, I told her that, but she said the rest of the village was there and we were 'conspicuous by our absence'."

"Bloody hell, so now I've got to go praying to keep in with Clay Hill, have I?"

Sue sighed. "Look, darling, it'll only be once a week. Sing a few hymns, smile at people and we'll be out in an hour. Anyway, Reverend Phillips has invited us to dinner tomorrow night."

"I'm playing darts with Tom tomorrow."

"Not anymore you're not."

"Sherry?" asked Reverend Phillips, a man of perhaps seventy, thin, ascetic, and quite bald.

"Just a small one for me," said Sue.

"I'll have a large one … please," I said, noticing Sue's disapproving look.

The reverend handed us glasses that looked like they were worth a few bob, filled with the pale nectar. "Ah, here's Mildred, my wife."

A large woman with a huge chest, dressed in black, came in. She had dark beady eyes and a round, greasy face. "Hello, Sue, and er ... it's Terence, isn't it?"

"That's right, but please call me Terry."

"Well, I hope you're both hungry, cook is doing us roast pheasant, with all the trimmings." She gave a laugh that sounded like a fox barking.

I sat down on a *chaise-long*. "Actually, I'm starving, I only had a couple of slices of toast and marmalade this morning."

She beamed, "Excellent. What is it you do, Terrence?"

"Oh, er, I'm a writer."

Mildred descended onto a brown leather armchair, leaning forward so that her ponderous bosom rested on her oversized knees. "How exciting! So what kind of thrilling tales do you write, Terence? Spy novels I suspect!"

"Actually, no, I write washing machine manuals."

She looked at me as if I'd just crawled out from under a stone. Thankfully the dinner bell rang.

We sat at a table set for five, the Reverend opposite me and Mildred opposite Sue. I nodded to the empty seat at the head of the table. "Who's joining us, then?"

No one said anything and there was an awkward silence. I felt my face flushing.

Fortunately, just then the door opened, and a servant entered with a food-laden trolley. She turned to Mildred. "Should I serve some out for the Colonel, ma'am?"

Mildred looked straight ahead. "That won't be necessary," she said tersely in a low voice.

The Colonel? Who the hell was that?

There was an impressive spread. First there was soup, a thin broth with pieces of what tasted like mutton floating around in it, then followed the pheasant, served with crisp roast potatoes, parsnips, broccoli, carrots, and half a dozen other vegetables, all cooked to *al dente* perfection.

Meanwhile, I eyed the empty chair, wondering …. "This is delicious," I said. "Your cook is a treasure."

"Thank you," said the reverend, leaning back in his chair and gazing fondly at the ceiling, "she is indeed a delight. Well, you know, it would have been back in, ah, 1962 when her mother first—"

"Quiet!" snapped Mildred, putting her knife and fork down. She sat back and her eyes seemed to roll around in her head until only the whites were showing. She sat bolt upright and shocked us by speaking in a deep male voice. "Greetings, friends, it is good to have you here. We send you blessings from all of us here in the Spirit World." She addressed Sue. "Yes, your father, Alex, is here, and … and June your sister."

I saw Sue's eyes water. "Hello, Dad, hello, sis."

Mildred's booming male voice continued. "You must not worry. Either of you. We are well here in the Spirit World and with you whenever you think of us. And Terence?"

"Er, yes?"

"Grandfather Jack says to stop wasting so much money on the lottery. The only way to get rich is through hard work."

Exactly the kind of thing he *would* say. I blushed but said nothing.

"And now friends, I leave you to enjoy your meal, and remember, the Great Spirit loves you all." With that, Mildred's eyes and posture returned to normal, and, as if nothing untoward had happened, she stabbed a hunk of pheasant, rolled it in gravy and brought it up to her cavernous mouth.

Sue and I exchanged glances. It looked like life in Clay Hill might not be so dull after all!

The Listening

John Gamble looked at his son, Ian, with pride. He'd grown into a fine young man, just started at a prestigious architectural company after his degree, and here he was with Gloria, his charming new girlfriend. John admired Gloria's long, chestnut hair, her perfect smile, appreciated her intelligent conversation, and, dare he admit it, even felt a touch of lust at the sight of her tight, well-filled blouse and figure-hugging blue jeans. "Thank you, Gloria, those figurines have been in the family a long time. Since I was a child in fact, and that *is* a long time!"

Mildred Gamble looked at her son and wondered how Ian, and, no doubt, her husband too, judging by the simpering expression on his aged face, could have fallen for this girl. Yes, she had the tits and arse, and Ian was a man after all, she acknowledged, with desires. Even she had felt those once. But he was good-looking, well qualified and on track for a bright future in architecture. Whereas, by all accounts, this girl worked in a record store, if there even were such things still, and had no family to speak of. "Yes, Gloria, dear, I believe they came from Great Aunt Fanny and were made in the time of Queen Anne, though I don't remember that myself!"

Gloria laughed politely. She wanted one thing, and that was to get upstairs to bed and for Ian to give her a good 'seeing to.' "Well, John, Mildred, thank you so much for a lovely meal. I think it's time for me to hit the sack. I've had a long day and I'm bushed …."

"I'm going to have a brandy, would you like one dear?" asked John, when Ian and Gloria had gone upstairs.

"I think I need one after that."

"What on earth do you mean, dear?"

"That awful girl, no ambition, no ideas of her own, just regurgitating sound-bites from so-called celebrities."

John returned with two brandy balloons, quarter-filled. "Well, I found her quite charming."

"*Pfft*. Nothing to do with her anatomy of course."

John blushed. "Well, er, I admit she's a bonny lass, but—"

"Listen, I've an idea."

"What."

"Well, they're in the east wing."

"And?"

"So, there's a baby monitor up there."

"So?"

"So, we could switch on the receiver and hear what they're saying."

"That's an awful idea. Mildred, I'm surprised at you. Anyway, it'll be turned off and even if it weren't, they'd see the red light."

Mildred gave a sly smile, "Not if 'someone' had turned it on and hidden it down the back of the sofa!"

All was quiet, just a slight hiss from the receiver. Mildred felt a stab of disappointment, John a feeling of relief. Then suddenly a giggle, and Gloria's voice. "Did you see his face when I said I liked Donald Trump, what a freak!"

"Oh, dad's not so bad."

John bristled.

"And your mum. The way she supports the establishment, believes all the lies they pump out on the telly and in the newspapers, silly cow!"

Mildred put her glass down with shaking hands.

"That's just her way, no need to criticise her. She means well."

"Well, if you ask me, they're a couple of arseholes. And to think I've got to put up with another two days of them."

"Just be nice, turn on the charm, like you did at dinner, it's only till Sunday and we can leave after lunch, if that's what you want."

"What I *want* is a good poke, and right now!"

There came more giggling and the sound of grunting. Mildred turned the receiver off and they sat staring at each other. John raised his eyebrows. "Well, it was your idea."

Mildred reminded John of a gasping fish. With an effort, she regained her voice, speaking hesitantly, "Well, … *perhaps* she has a point. We sit in front of the goggle-box and never question what we're told."

"And we poo-poo anyone who says different," admitted John.

"Look, do me a favour."

"What?"

Mildred gave a wry smile. "Pour me another brandy."

"OK, dear."

"Then take me upstairs and give me a good poke!"

Danny and the Dolly Bird

Fleetwood Mac was playing quietly on the CD player when Danny Golightly walked into Seddon's Estate Agents. The song was *Dreams*. Danny remembered his parents smooching to it in the living room. He'd been embarrassed at the time. His step faltered as he acknowledged the irony of the song title.

"Can I help you, sir?"

It was an older man, not one of the 'dolly birds' who normally grace the teak-veneered desks of such establishments. He had long grey sideburns, silver rimmed glasses, short grey hair, cut neatly with a side-parting, and a look of resignation. A desk sign said 'Mr. Jack Seddon,' followed by a string of post-nominal initials.

Danny looked around. 'I'd like a house, a big one with a garden, trees, that sort of thing."

Seddon looked the youth up and down. Skinny blue jeans, black loafers, a black T-shirt with the logo *FCUK* and a black leather jacket that looked like it had previously belonged to a hell-raising 'Rock 'n' Roller' – or two. "I see, sir, and are you a first-time buyer?"

"Yeah."

Seddon sighed. "And you have the wherewithal?"

Danny looked nonplussed. "What's that?"

Seddon sat upright with the fingers of both hands pressed together, the fingernails turning white. "The funds to buy a property!"

"Oh, er, yeah."

"Well, may I ask what you are thinking of, er, ah, spending?"

Danny scanned around the photographs of properties for sale. His eye caught a white house with a tall, arched window on the first floor. Extensions grew out on both sides, terminating in a conservatory at the west end and a summer house and garage at the east side. A stone monument stood on a patio, a small-scale replica of Cleopatra's Needle. The view was taken from some distance away across a huge lawn, bordered by violet hydrangeas. The notice said, The Julian Granger House. "Hey, I like this one!" he exclaimed.

Seddon looked at his watch. Where on earth was Miss Hale? She should be taking care of this nonsense. "That house is £695,000, sir. Are you sure that's in your, er, price range?"

"Are there any trees?"

Seddon pulled out a brochure. A view taken across the lawn from wooden decking in front of the house showed a group of mature elms and beeches on the far side He tapped the photograph brusquely. "Perhaps you'd like to take this brochure and think about it. We could arrange a viewing ... possibly."

Danny's face remained impassive but inside he was ecstatic. This house looked perfect. He'd have a pool table in the conservatory and one of the many rooms the Julian Granger House sported could house his drum kits. And there'd be no neighbours to annoy by the looks of things. "Er, yeah, I'll take it!"

Seddon sighed. "Look, sir, it's not like buying a can of beans, you know. The place has to be surveyed, there are forms to be filled, solicitors to deal with, they're not philanthropists, they all want their pound of ... er, their cut."

Danny reached into his jacket and pulled out a pink slip of paper. He put it on the desk in front of Seddon. The latter's eyes narrowed. "Look, Mr. Seddon, this ticket's worth two million quid. Look, you can check the numbers and the date."

"How do I know it's real," asked Seddon cautiously.

"Feel it. You know it is."

"Well, that's good news then! Claim your prize and come to me with a bank statement showing you have the funds and we can proceed."

Danny sighed. "Look, Mr. Seddon, I don't want none of that. I can't be bothered with bank accounts and such. I'll give you this ticket. *You* cash it in. You give me a million quid in cash, sort the house out in my name and you can keep the rest."

Seddon gasped. "Now, listen young man, I don't mean to be discourteous, but ... but you can't be serious, surely?"

"I am, Mr. Seddon, I am."

Seddon took the pink slip. It was slightly creased but the print was clear as day. He reached over to his desktop keyboard and pulled up the National Lottery website. He clicked on Check

Results and typed in the numbers. He almost fell off his chair. The prize was two million, ninety thousand. An extra ninety grand for nothing! Trying to keep his breath even and steady, he looked up at the young man. "Yes, er, I think that would be in order. Mr. er?"

"Golightly, Danny Golightly. And I want the cash in twenties and tens, a hundred boxes, ten grand a box, OK?"

"Well, er, certainly, sir ... as you desire."

A bell rang above the door and a young woman entered. "Sorry I'm late sir, just there was a bunch of wild geese on the road. Can you believe it? They wouldn't budge for no one!"

"Actually, Miss Hale, I *do* find that hard to believe. Why didn't you just drive over them?"

"What, and get prosecuted for cruelty to animals!"

"They're not animals, they're birds!"

"Same difference ... sir." She suddenly noticed Danny standing there, looking amused. She looked him up and down, approvingly.

Seddon stood up. "Miss Hale, I'd like you to meet Mr. Golightly. He's interested in the Julian Granger House. Could you arrange to show him around please? *Now* would be a good time!"

Danny looked at Miss Hale. About thirty, ten years on him, but tall, slim, long ash-blonde hair, heavyish up top, not especially pretty but attractive, wearing black-framed glasses. No rings on her fingers neither. *Whoa*, a dolly bird in glasses! That did it for him; he felt like all his Christmases had come at once.

As Seddon watched them leave, he made a quick calculation. At Miss Hale – Freda's – current rate of three hundred pounds a night, he'd be able to afford thirteen hundred more nights with her! That was, hmm, just over ten years at three times a week, the maximum Dolores would believe his tale of 'working down in Devon.' At his age, that was probably the most he could manage anyway, even with Viagra. He wasn't worried about Danny; he'd move on to younger and better-looking birds. He picked up the lottery ticket and pressed his lips to it, imagining it was a certain part of Freda's anatomy. He was awoken from his reverie by the shop bell ringing again. He looked up, startled. "Delores, er, hello, my dear, what a nice, er … surprise."

A mottled hand with pincer-like red nails snatched the ticket out of his grip.

Tranquil Beginnings

End of life is never easy, Alfred Marwood thought. But at least he could have the television as loud as he liked now, without Susan's nagging. "The televisions a bit loud, Alfred, can't you turn it down?" And then there was the dishwasher. He'd never known there was a *wrong* way to empty it before Susan. And come to think of it, there were a dozen other things he'd miss about his wife like a hole in the head. He sighed and knocked on the door.

Susan Marwood did not leave a great deal of money when she died, and her will was a simple one. With the exception of a few small bequests to relatives, she left all her property to her husband.

Mr. Atchity, the solicitor, and Alfred Marwood went over Susan's will together in the solicitor's office, and when the business was completed, the widower got up to leave. At that point, the solicitor took a sealed envelope from a folder on his desk and held it out to his client. "I've been instructed to give you this," he said. "Your wife sent it to us shortly before she passed away."

Alfred took the bulky envelope, wondering what on earth was in it? Perhaps Susan wanted to tell him – in retrospect – that she'd loved him, that he'd been a good husband to her, maybe even to apologize for her constant nagging and criticism of him? Well, that'd be something, he thought, as he bade the solicitor good day and made his way out of the office.

Back home, Alfred put the envelope on the mantlepiece and poured himself out a whisky, something Susan had always chided him for. Damn it, he'd have a large one, he thought, adding an extra splash and some ice.

Alfred turned the television on and was pleased to see there was football. Chelsea versus Everton. He turned the volume up nice and loud and settled back in his chair. He enjoyed the company of the crowd roaring and singing. But somehow, he found he couldn't enjoy the game. His mind and eye were constantly drawn to the envelope on the mantlepiece. Finally, he could stand it no more. He got up, snapped the television off and took Susan's letter down. He sat at the table and slit the envelope open. Then he began to read, his jaw dropping progressively towards the floor.

Dear Alfred, well, if you are reading this you'll have seen Mr. Atchity and he'll have gone over the will with you. I'm sure you'll be happy with the arrangements.

Well, you know I was going to Tranquil Beginnings, the therapists, for my little 'problem,' something I have to say you were not in the slightest bit supportive of. But that's over and done with now I suppose, now that I'm dead, so to speak.

Anyway, the woman, June, who saw me, told me how she treats people whose souls have fragmented and bits have left the body, sometimes even gone to hide, can you believe? That's when the person has undergone something extremely traumatic, she says.

Well, June told me she had one client who hadn't got a soul! Extremely unusual apparently but there we are, it had just up and gone, and they couldn't find it anywhere!

Of course, I didn't mention any of this to you, you'd just have pooh-poohed it in your usual way. But then she told me how they could transfer my soul to this poor person after my death. It was all rather complicated and I won't bore you here with the details, Alfred. But it means that, although my body will die from this ghastly cancer, the real part of me, the part where my personality and memories reside, will live on in a new body. Isn't it thrilling, Alfred?

So, you just need to phone Tranquil Beginnings to find out how it all went, and I'll be back home in a jiffy!

By the way, dear, do you really need to have the television so loud? You know it's not good for your ears. And you really should cut down on the whisky too. It's not good for your heart, you know ....

Alfred put the letter down without reading further, feeling quite cross. Just a list of other instructions and complaints. Maybe he'd look at them later, or maybe he wouldn't. And what on earth was all this hogwash about Susan having her soul transferred to a new woman. Was such a thing even possible? Surely not. He poured himself out another whisky, not quite so large this time, and added two cubes of ice.

Hmm, he wondered whether to phone Tranquil Beginnings and ask their advice? Pah, it was all nonsense! He turned the television on again and settled back to watch the match. Presently the doorbell rang. Who the hell was that? Alfred got up with annoyance and proceeded to the door, opening it to a large brute of a man with a pronounced belly and a beard.

"Yes, can I help you."

"Alfred, dear, it's me, Susan," said the man, beaming. He stepped forward and embraced Alfred, kissing him on the lips.

Alfred pulled away. "What. Get off!"

"Don't worry, Alfred, dear, you'll get used to my new appearance, and, by the way, the television's a bit loud you know, *and* you've been drinking whisky again!"

Never Lovelier

It was a beautiful day, thought Mr. FtF as he sat on the patio with his newspaper waiting for his wife to come down. Why did it always take her so long to get ready in the morning, he wondered? All that ... preening! He put his paper down and gazed at the canal that flowed past the bottom of their garden. Purple liquid sparkled in the light of the two suns in a way that never ceased to amaze Mr. FtF. It depended on their positions relative to each other he supposed, as he sipped his *kaffa*.

The canal was wide, twenty times as wide as their house, he'd once calculated, and theirs was a big house too, a grand affair on many levels fabricated from clear plastic. He liked the way passersby on the canal could see their expensive furniture, pictures and ornaments, not least the life-size statue of the Great Ruler, carved from a rare and precious green stone.

"Good morning, Mr. FtF."

He looked up at his wife. "Why, Mrs. FtF, you look lovely today! The *kaffa's* hot and there's toasted *fragen*. Come and join me."

Mrs. FtF, sat down. She loved the way she could feel warmth on her front and back at the same time and watch the canal flowing slowly past, in no hurry to go anywhere. "Anything in the paper, Mr. FtF?"

"Hah. Look at this!" He held up the newspaper to show a picture of some kind of craft.

"What is it?" she asked.

"A goddamned rocket ship can you believe! That's what this addle-brained government want to build!"

Mrs. FtF poured a cup of *kaffa* and spread a slice of *fragen* with a creamy blue paste.

"Well, they must have a reason."

"Reason be damned!" exclaimed Mr. FtF. "They say they're going to fire it into space!"

"Where would it go, and who would drive it?"

"That's just the point, Mrs. FtF, there *is* nowhere to go! As to who would *pilot* it, airmen would be specially trained."

Mrs. FtF felt excited. "Maybe they'll find some new people out ... out in space!"

"Don't be ridiculous. Our scientists have scoured the sky with the best telescopes ever built. Looked out to other galaxies even. No sign of anyone! In any case, the Great Ruler says that GdG created the universe specially for us, here on this planet."

Mrs. FtF stood up and bowed her head. "Praise be to GdG." Then she sat down again.

"Anyway, where are they going to get the money to build this thing?" asked Mr. FtF, rhetorically.

"Good morning Mr. FtF, good morning Mrs. FtF!" It was their neighbour, Mr. DnD, sailing past on his silver sail-boat. He pulled into the bank, tied the sail-boat and walked up their garden path. "You're looking lovely today, Mrs. FtF, if I may say so!"

Mrs. FtF felt a flush of pride. "Why thank you Mr. DnD, and, yes, you may say so!"

They all laughed. "Come and join us," said Mr. FtF.

Mr. DnD sat down and Mrs. FtF poured him some *kaffa* and spread some *fragen*.

"I suppose you've heard about this crazy space ship idea?" asked Mr. FtF.

"Well, my son works for the government, as you know, so I've been hearing about it for a while. But I'll tell you something you don't know. Where they're going to get the money from."

"Where's that then?" Mr. FtF asked. But Mr. DnD seemed in no hurry to spill the beans, chewing his *fragen*, sipping *kaffa* and gazing at the leisurely-flowing purple canal.

"Come on, Mr DnD," said Mrs. FtF. "Out with it. Don't keep us in suspense!"

"Clothes, Mrs. FtF. That's where it's coming from. Clothes, they're going to tax our clothes!"

"Tax our clothes. How will they do that? I've never heard of anything so ridiculous!" exclaimed Mr. FtF.

"Well, a government inspector will call round and count your clothing items. You'll pay one percent of a unit per month for each clothing item."

Mr. FtF made an exasperated gesture. "Well, Mrs. FtF's going to cost me about …" He made a quick calculation "… about three units a month!" He turned to his wife. "Right Mrs. FtF, tomorrow I'm going to take half your clothes to the tip. So, you'd better get started sorting!"

Mrs. FtF pulled a face. "What about you, Mr. FtF, all those old shirts that don't fit you anymore! All that *fragen* you eat!"

"Pah," exclaimed Mr. FtF.

"Anyway, Mr. DnD, what about gloves, does each one count as a clothing item?" asked Mrs. FtF anxiously.

"Don't worry, Mrs. FtF," smiled Mr DnD, "each *set* counts as one item."

Mrs. FtF got up. "Excuse me, I just need to er, powder my face." She went indoors, both hearing and seeing the men arguing about the relative values of firing a rocket ship into space. Whoever heard of such a thing, she thought? She went into the bathroom, reached out a tentacle for a towel and wiped her forehead. She admired herself in the mirror, where her five eyes blinked back. She felt so happy she could feel drool spilling from her beak. Yes, she did indeed look lovely today!

The Magic Roundabout

Lambda could see the lights of the supermarket through the shrubbery and across the canal, but here, on the pathway to the road, it was sparsely lit, and the adjoining children's play area was dark and desolate. He looked around, then, with no one in sight, leapt over the six-foot fence and sat on the roundabout. He took a key ring out and played with the cold metals, toying with ideas. Finally, randomly flicking through them, 'Fuck it,' he thought. Holding one tight he began to kick the ground, the roundabout spinning in response. "Make the connection. Make the connection!"

Round and round. Round and round, then ... he was in a colossal room with stone walls. The floor was earthen and there were gigantic wooden benches and tables. Huge logs blazed in an enormous fireplace, throwing out sparks like twinkling fireflies.

The floor began to vibrate, and something began to approach. Thud ... thud ... thud. A deep voice began to boom out. "Fee Fi Fo Fum."

Lambda quickly flicked through the key ring to the glowing silver 'home' key. Gripping it tightly, he began the mantra, "Make the connection ..."

Wham, he was back on the roundabout, which was now slowly coming to a halt. He breathed a sigh of relief. Why waste precious energy fighting an evil giant?

But at the back of his mind whirled thoughts of Jack and the Golden Goose. No, he must help elsewhere. Once more he selected a key, this time a tiny brass one. "Make the connection ..."

He found himself on a vast concrete walkway, surrounded by skyscrapers. Around him were beings, they looked human, all walking the same way as him, but engrossed with small silver screens. Reflected in a ground floor window he could see himself in a red leather jacket, the others, intent on their anonymous journeys, clad in sombre blacks and browns. Then the sky went dark. Lambda looked up to see an enormous black disc above, blotting out the sky. Surprisingly, no one around him seemed to take any notice.

With one giant leap for mankind, he flew to the top of a skyscraper. There he could look directly into a lens at the bottom of the craft. Some kind of device was being readied. The kind of device that would vaporise the 'zombies' below, he surmised. He reached into his jacket for a small metal sphere, then into another pocket for a launcher. With practised precision he launched the nuclear seed right into the centre of the lens.

Without waiting for the fallout, literally, he once again grasped the home key. "Make the connection …"

Back on the roundabout, he noticed an approaching couple and quickly turned on his invisibility shield, hearing them laughing and swearing as they passed. He looked over at the supermarket lights. Life could be exciting as a Super Hero but he needed to eat, after all. Deciding to leave the worlds to their problems he headed to the hot chicken counter.

When the Fat Man Croaks

"Death, I am not keen on, overmuchly," said Donut Dave, turning a funny shade of yellow.

"Well, I'm only passin' on what I heard last night at Max's," I said. "Seems Big Cyril and da boys is out lookin' for you. On account of you visitin' Missy Cymbeline Banks, Cyril's best gal."

"Sure, I seen her, but only to measure her up for a trombone, says she wants to learn in secret like, give Cyril and the boys a big surprise at the club one night."

Donut was a hot jazz piano player, so I guessed there was some truth in his story. "Well, the way I hear it, Cyril's gotta surprise in mind for *you*, he's gonna be measurin' *you* up – for a pair of concrete pyjamas!"

There was a knock on the door and Donut looked around frantically for somewhere to hide.

"Relax oneself," I said, "it'll only be Suzie Spade, the maid." I opened the door to a lady as black as her name and a smile like a polished banana.

"Hullo, Mister Paul, and you, Mister. ... er, David." She looked sheepish. "I wasn't expectin' to see you alive again, truth to tell."

Donut turned an even funnier shade of yellow.

"Can you start upstairs?" I asked.

"Sure, Mister Paul, I start in the bathroom. Polishin' them tiles till I can see my dimples! By the way, d'you hear Massa Noble in town? You know, that one who owns all them bettin' shops, swans around town like he owns the place!"

I laughed. "Actually, he does own most of it! Jackie Noble, he's OK, in fact he's kind of a friend of mine."

"I never knew that," chimed up Donut, wiping the sweat off his brow with a tea towel, like a barman mopping up spilt beer. "How come?"

"Well," I said, "it's all on account of when he was starting up. He'd only been set up a week when there was a big race, the Silverstone Derby, and that kid up at the Hartman stables, we used to call him the Humbug Kid, on account of a bag of humbugs he always had, stickying up a pocket, plus all the 'humbug' he used to talk. Anyways, he gives me a 'sure fire bet' on a donkey named Northwest Passage. I said, 'You gotta be kiddin' me, 'Bug. That nag wouldn't win if the rest of them hosses ran backwards!' But he took on a serious kinda look, somethin' you saw less than a peanut-hawker in the White House, and he says, 'Mister Paul,' trust me on this."

"And what happened then?" asked Suzie.

"You still here!" I said. "Well, for Pete's sake, the front two hosses fell and ol' Northwest Passage rolled in, in first place! Well, it would practically have bankrupted Jackie Noble, the amount I'd bet, so I reached an 'agreement' with him and let him off."

There was another knock on the door. We all jumped, then breathed a sigh of relief as it opened to Jazzy Jay the trumpeter and his side-kick, Sonny Bones the drummer.

"Hi Y'all," exclaimed Jazzy, putting down a trumpet case and taking off shades blacker than a coalminer's doo dah. "Hey, Donut, I hear from Missy Cymbeline Banks that you sortin' out a trombone for her, in an ambiguous kind o' way." He laughed. "Well, I've come to offer some advice. You see, she gonna be playin' a lot in the key of B flat, so what she wants is—"

Well, we never did hear what she wanted as just then there came yet another knock on the door. Sonny Bones pulled out some drumsticks and began a crescendo on a nearby sideboard. Before I could complain, the door crashed open and there stood Big Cyril, flanked by Johnny 'Knuckleduster' Norris and Herman 'Gravedigger' Hemmings, with baby-faced little Sammy Poison bringing up the rear.

Cyril squeezed through the doorway with a violin case, shadowed by his henchmen. "Hey Donut. I gotta matter to settle wit' you. You been messin' with my Cymbeline." He put the violin case on a piano and extracted a Tommy Gun.

"You crazy?" exclaimed Donut, "everyone'll hear and they'll talk."

Cyril gave a sarcastic laugh. "Ever'one within earshot will hear, no one'll talk, not if they wanna spend the rest of their lives breathin'." He aimed the gun at Donut's chest. "And it'll act as a ... as a kinda warning. People gotta show me veneration."

Without thinking, I grabbed the barrel, just as a deafening burst of bullets tore into the carpet.

"What ... you!" exclaimed Cyril. "You're next in line for a lead tuxedo!"

"No, listen," I said, "how'd you and da boys, Knuckleduster and Gravedigger here, and little Sammy Poison too, like a no-expenses Caribbean Cruise on a luxury liner, *The Beautician*?"

Cyril frowned, "Hey, that's part-owned by Jackie Noble ain't it?"

I reached into my jacket and pulled out a yellowing letter. "See, signed by Jackie Noble."

Cyril read it, then the penny dropped. He smiled. "Well, boys, I guess we could use a little sun, and my Cymbeline'd sure look cute in a bikini! Boys, go down to Maxie's, bring us up a few bottles ... and a few gals. We're gonna have us a party right here! Jazzy and Sunny, get groovin' and you, fat boy," he gestured towards Donut, "get tinklin' them ivories!"

All Apologies (A Writers' A-Z)

A – Audiobooks

"What, little me have an audiobook published? You gotta be kiddin'!" Or words to that effect. But why not? If you've managed to publish something on Amazon (see Y) register your title with ACX and wait [patiently] for the auditions to roll in. With a split-royalty deal you won't even have to pay a penny upfront either!

B – Belief in Yourself

This is important, up to a point. But can you actually, really, honestly, I mean, when push comes to shove – write? Have you had good feedback from other writers, competition judges etc. or is your knowledge of spelling, grammar, punctuation, manuscript layout and all the rest of it, like a pile of poo? If so, there's no need to throw yourself under the nearest trolley-bus. You *still* have a story to tell. Everyone does. Record it on audio and find a ghost-writing buddy (or employ someone if you are a Billy No Mates type) to turn it into the latest smash-hit feelgood autobiography/screenplay/TV series.

C – Computer Problems

How many times have you heard this one? Computers are so cheap now, second-hand ('used') under a hundred quid, it's sometimes easier to stop throwing money down the drain on repairs to your top-of-the-range MacBook Pro and buy yourself a cheapo Windows laptop instead. Microsoft Professional Plus 2016 (including Word) could be had for under £15 on Amazon! At least you'll be able to write again.

If it's a case of software problems, I've found it's usually 'operator error.' Get someone who knows what they are doing to look at the problem(s) with you. And you could always look at the manual (if there is one), you know!

D – Dogs

'I have to take the dog for a walk' is a common excuse. OK, fair enough, your little pooch needs to stretch its littler legs from time to time. As well as poo on the grass, pee on fences and sniff other dogs' bums. But while your mutt is doing those mundane doggy-matters, you could be listening to an audiobook on writing. Sol Stein's one takes some beating. So, you could be brushing up on 'show versus tell' and 'points of view' whilst dear little Fido is running around fetching sticks or peeing on (more) fences.

E – Editing

Just like a carpenter can knock out a table in five minutes (maybe a bit longer) they will then spend HOURS sanding, planing, polishing and whatever else carpenters do. It's the same with us wordsmiths, one can knock out a short story in half an hour or so (assuming you can type properly. You can, right?) but then it might take one to two hours in total (or more) to spruce it up. Ditto a short chapter or a scene.

Look, the eagle-eyed reader will immediately spot typos, repeated words, redundant phrases, mistakes, words you've used before in close proximity – you get the idea. So, it pays to learn to enjoy editing and get good at it!

Second draft = first draft – 10%, so says Stephen King (although maybe a case of 'Do as I say …?') but it'll tighten up the writing as well as weed out the evils above. Whether third draft = second draft – 10% etc. he didn't say.

Marcy Kennedy's books are a help too.

Also, many report that it's easier to edit than it is to write from scratch when you are tired.

F – First Draft

"I'm afraid my first draft won't be any good."

"First drafts aren't *supposed* to be any good, just write and let the creative juices flow (you idiot)!"

You can sort out all the typos and clunkiness later. As someone once said, 'You can't edit a blank page.' Kudos to that man!

G – Grandkids

(One for the 'silver surfer' generation) See K – Kids below.

H – Hiatus

"I'm stuck on my book."

A common excuse. But it doesn't stop you writing something else in the interim – could be short stories, poetry, memoirs, etc.

K M Weiland's books are pretty useful for unsticking yourself too.

N.B. the plural of *hiatus* is *hiatuses or hiatus* – for those sitting there, smirking to themselves, thinking the author had got it wrong.

I – Ill Health

"I have back pain/arm pain/wrist pain/no hands (etc.) and can't physically write."

Why are you reading a list of apologies for not writing then?!

J – Judge's Criticism

You've just had your lovely competition manuscript returned with a scathing critique that your dialogue isn't natural, there's no characterization, the plot is non-existent/terrible and the ending is awful. What can you do? The most useful tactic is to put your head under a pillow and cry for two hours. After you've recovered – this may take several days/weeks, but therapy is normally *not* required – read the judge's notes again with a clear, calm head, reminding yourself that they were just trying to give well-meaning advice.

Then, 1. Scream long and loud. 2. Decide to give up writing forever. 3. Change your mind and decide to improve in one area targeted by the kind-hearted judge for your next earth-shattering entry. Repeat for five to ten years until you *finally* get on the shortlist.

K – Kids

Noisy, demanding, irritating little buggers, and that's just their friends. Seriously, this is a biggie. You have to find some 'me time,' either when they are at school or by insisting that you are not disturbed. Well, you can live in hope. Or get up two hours earlier than them – that's what's recommended by some writers (ones who don't have kids).

L – Love

"I love you with so much of my heart that none is left to protest." Forsooth. You're madly in love and you can't possibly write anything other than love letters, love poems etc. etc. Don't worry, dear, forget about writing anything else for now, until it all fizzles out (it will).

M – Madness

Possibly conducive to becoming a writer in the first place but unlikely to contribute to useful relationships with industry bods – or sales, for that matter. Seek treatment. (See also L – Love above).

N – Nowhere to Write

Get in the car, drive to a park, the countryside, Tesco car park (as a last resort), open the windows for fresh air (except in Tesco car park) and do twenty minutes on your laptop. If you haven't got a laptop you can scribble on paper. Like what Shakespeare did.

If you haven't got a car, see K – Kids above.

O – Old Habits

Die hard. Like putting two spaces after a full-stop ('period' for our transatlantic friends). Look, the typewriter died out fifty years ago (give or take) and little things like that drive (some) editors and readers nuts. So, get with it, dear!

P – Punctuation

"I don't know how to do commas and stuff!"

"Well, there's this thing called the internet …."

And/or go to Amazon or your local [charity] bookshop and buy a book on punctuation and *read it*!

(See also O above)

Q – Quitting

Sometimes when you're writing and things ain't going so well, it's time to just pull the plug and quit. Fixing those clunky phrases and bits of dialogue that no one would *ever* say won't seem so foreboding in the clear light of the morrow.

N.B. Quitting should come at the *end* of a writing session, *not* the beginning.

R – Reading

Recommended by most writers (Stephen King is big on it). Otherwise, how do you know what 'good writing' is? But reading can become an excuse to not actually *write* anything. Ditto talking about writing, dreaming about writing, wishing you were writing ….

But, y'know, it pays to spend *some* time reading books *about* writing. Sol Stein says that writing is unusual in that some are reluctant to learn – or oblivious to – the *craft* of writing. Check out *Solutions for Writers* by SS for the lowdown.

S – Social Media

Yes, we all want to see what our friends are up to and gape at videos of pussycats climbing up poles and jumping down onto targets etc. Facebook is great but it won't progress your short story or novel will it? Ditto Twitter and the rest of 'em.

T – Time

"If I only had time, only time …" (feel free to warble along, fans of John Rowles). Together with Writers' Block this is the biggie. 'I don't have time,' cry countless wannabee writers. You never hear them crying, 'I can't be bothered,' or 'I don't have the talent,' or 'I don't have the patience.'

As an instrumental music teacher for over twenty years, the author has heard a boatful of excuses for not practising, very, *very* few of which have been valid.

And how much time do you actually need? Well, you can write something worthwhile in fifteen minutes. Fifteen minutes a day is one hour 45 minutes a week, 7.58333… hours a month …. You get the idea. And guess what? There'll be days when you can do *more* than fifteen minutes!

"How do I find fifteen minutes then?" you [may] ask.

In four words – TURN THE TELEVISION OFF!

U – Underscoring

Those nice red marks put in by well-meaning (but mean) judges and editors to curb your verbosity and highlight howling errors. Bite the bullet and take their advice. They've been at it longer than you, and you know what? They know what's what.

V - Vocabulary

"My vocabulary's too limited!"

Well, is there anyone who doesn't like Ray Bradbury? Oh, there is. Oh, well the author is not one of them (although he never could get past page two of *Dandelion Wine*). But you know what? Good 'ol Ray (hope he wouldn't have minded the familiar address) didn't go in for long, complicated and obscure words (*a la* Edgar Allen Poe). He used a relatively limited vocabulary, but, *ahh*, did he know how to use those words!

Indeed, Shakespeare was pretty much like that, even though 'half the words are in crummy old English,' to quote a nincompoop on the internet! [Actually, *Elizabethan English!*]

But if you *do* want to expand your vocabulary, sign up for Dictionary.com's 'word of the day' (and etymology thereof).

Finding synonyms for words you already know is a help too. Use a thesaurus online (or a good old-fashioned book, if you insist) to find a substitute word per day that you are unfamiliar with. List and keep using those new words. In three years, you'll have a thousand new words (at least) ready to spring to your adroit grey matter and lissom digits.

W – Writers' Block

Well, the granddaddy of all reasons to hold fire on putting pen (or pencil) to paper, or fingers to keyboard. Seems to refer to a general inability to think of what to put down on paper/screen.

Well, as Della Galton says in her *Short Story Writers' Toolshed*, she's never come across anyone with secretary's block, gardener's block or washer-upper's block. So why is writing special?

Answer, it isn't. You just have to use a bit of initiative. It's no good sitting staring at a blank screen or piece of A4. [Puts knotted handkerchief on head, adopts ape-like stance and shouts in best 'Gumby' voice] Blimey! I mean, blimey! ... blimey! [ad nauseum] Blimey ... I ... mean ... you've ... got ... to ... have ... an ...idea ... of ... what ... to ... write! Blimey ... it ... stands ... to ... reason. [Thank you, professor J.M. Gumby*]

How hard is that? There are thousands of ideas on the internet, plus countless books and magazines on writing. Or try the universal prompt recommended in practically every writing book going – *What if?*

Here goes ... er ... What if a man goes to sleep and wakes up to find he's been transformed into a giant insect! Whaddya mean, that one's already been had?! OK, OK, let's have another go. Er ... What if a man goes to a school reunion and everyone is curiously offhand with him .... There, that took under ten seconds. What happens and how does it end? Haven't a clue! Get writing with that idea and you'll soon find out! About two to three thousand words should do it. Perfect for the monthly *Writers' Forum* Story Contest. I mean ... *Blimey!*

*appears, courtesy of *Monty Python's Flying Circus*

X – X-rays

OK, OK, yes, very predictable I know. But Xylophone Practice didn't seem so appropriate and, anyway, Patrick Moore managed to do pretty well, writing an impressive 112 tomes whilst doing so. Not to mention endless tours telling us for the million + nth time that the Sun goes around the Earth, or is it the other way around? I can never remember.

Anyway, yes, X-ray appointments plus general out-patient and in-patient appointments *do* interfere with daily writing practice, it has to be admitted. But, hey, waiting rooms are a damn good source of characters and story ideas if you keep your eyes and ears open. Well, perhaps not ears so much; some people don't seem capable of talking in anything less than a shout. (See also W – Writer's Block above).

Y – Yttrium

Only joking! Y is *really* for *Why* are you not a published author? Seriously, it's simple now to self-publish on Kindle. All you need is a measly 2500 words or so. And it's not that much harder to publish a paperback (although you'll likely need a few more words). Check out https://kdp.amazon.com/.

Bear in mind, however, that self-publishing and actually *selling* your cherished efforts are like calcium carbonate and *fromage*.

Z - Zzzz

That moment when you can't see the text for the red squiggles that Word so helpfully puts in, and your head starts to droop. Time to call it quits. Tomorrow's another day.

Animal Magic

"David's deer, where are they, mate?"

A man in a dark-green top and blue trousers stopped his work, brushing the floor of an animal enclosure. He eyed the young man – clad in dirty jeans and a grey hoodie – disapprovingly, "*Père* David's deer, oh, they're on loan for a few days."

"Well, they weren't here last week neither. The bloke on duty said they were sleeping."

The zoo keeper sighed. "Well, animals have to sleep!"

A girl with blonde hair in a pony tail joined them, linking arms with the young man. "Well, I went to see the giraffes and there was only one, in a smelly building. None out in the paddock."

The keeper began to brush the floor once more. "Well, what do expect me to do about it?"

The girl continued. "And I went to see the lions, just one, lying down, it might as well have been stuffed! What do you say, Steve?"

The young man looked around at the paddocks, pavilions and thinly-populated walkways. "Well, I don't see a whole lot of animals, mate. I thought this was supposed to be one of the top zoos in the country. I reckon I saw more animals in that musical, *Cats*!"

The keeper stopped brushing and leant his broom against a wall. He approached the young couple. Glancing around to make sure none of the paltry crowd of visitors was within earshot, he lowered his voice. "Look, the truth is, this zoo's going downhill – and *fast*. Time was when we had *herds* of Père David's Deer, a dozen lions, polar bears, even a herd of Euclid's gazelle. But people are funny, kind of gone off zoos, 'cruel to animals' you hear them say, all this 'political correctness' gone mad. So, they don't bring their kiddies so much nowadays. There used to be throngs of the little buggers in the old days, all shouting and screaming at the animals. Now it's all about getting visitors into the gift shop and cinema and museum."

"Well, we came to see animals," exclaimed the young woman. "You know, furry things that move around on their own!"

The keeper sighed. "Look, I understand. Do you think I want to spend my time, brushing an empty paddock, putting out imported dung to make it look like animals were here?"

Steve turned to the girl. "Come on, Sue, I'm going to blow the whistle on this lot." He turned to the keeper, "So where do I find the general manager, I'd like a little word with him first."

Behind the refectory, gift shop, museum and cinema, was a small drab building. It housed the manager of the Royal Park Zoo. A sign on the door said 'Hugo Charles,' followed by a long string of initials, in which the letter Z was prominent. Mr Charles himself sat behind an expansive mahogany desk, a desk that matched his appearance – overweight and red-faced. "Look, I'm sorry, Steve and er, ... Sue. It seems you've been 'had.' That fellow you spoke to was an imposter."

Steve and Sue exchanged glances. "Whaddya mean, an imposter!" Steve exclaimed, "He was wearing a uniform."

The manager sighed, "Well, did it have any lettering on it? RPZ for example?"

"Well, no it never, come to think of it," said Sue.

"Precisely! This fellow, Wentworth Biggins, is, well, not to put it too finely, a loony, someone who comes here solely to spread malicious rumours. On account of his objection to keeping animals in captivity. As if the precious work we do—"

"He said you put down fake dung," interrupted Sue.

"Ah, yes, he says all kinds of things. That the crocodiles and hippos are just mechanical heads on sticks that bob up and down at random intervals, that the lions are stuffed, the zebras are just ponies with stripes painted on them! All kinds of nonsense. I can assure you we have *hundreds* of real live animals."

Steve stood up, pulling his hood over his head. "Come on, Sue, seems we were wrong."

Mr Charles stood up, likewise, smiling and brandishing two tickets. "Look, I'm so sorry for the misunderstanding. Here are two annual tickets. Free entry to the museum, gift shop and cinema, with my complements. I can promise plenty of entertainment!"

Once the couple had left, Mr Charles picked up the phone. "Hello, James, it's Hugo. Look, Perkins has been talking out of turn again, that man is a positive menace, just *cannot* keep a secret. Get him to clean out the tigers, will you? ... Yes, and is there some way you can fix it so they can get back in when he's cleaning ... ah, excellent!" Satisfied, Mr Charles took a magazine, *Zoo Supplies Weekly*, down from a shelf and turned to the 'dung for sale' pages.

Pie in the Sky

Sergeant Rowena Martens stood five feet three inches in her stockinged feet and weighed one hundred pounds almost exactly. Despite her petite size she was strong, fast, and had a talent that gave the men in her platoon quite a surprise when first encountered.

She was twenty-four years old and from the city of Mountain View in California, where her parents' extensive house and gardens gazed up at the Santa Cruz mountains, and where she'd discovered an aptitude for rock climbing.

Her father, Heinz, was a German who had worked on V-rockets in the war and subsequently found a niche at NASA and then in Silicon Valley. The fact that he'd been a member of the Nazi party and, through his rocket designs, responsible for thousands of deaths was dismissed, like someone brushing a few crumbs from their jacket lapel.

Rowena had the same quick intelligence, and when her friend, Natalie, said she wanted to join the army, her surprise gave way to acceptance and then enthusiasm to do likewise, to everyone's amazement.

Natalie opted for the Finance Corps as a 'cushy option.' Rowena applied to the Signal Corps, and, in the time before joining, worked on her physical fitness and fighting skills.

"Well, lookee here, we've got ourselves a midget!" laughed Tanner Sutherland, standing behind her in the dinner queue on her first day.

Rowena turned around. "Well, lookee here, we've got ourselves an ugly moron!"

There was laughter and a few soldiers gathered around to watch the scene. Tanner's face was red with rage. "There shouldn't be no women in our army, especially not little shortarses, you'd be no good in close combat."

Rowena pulled out of the queue and stood facing Tanner, balancing lightly on the balls of her feet.

"Hey, lay off her, Tanner," said Norton Breakspear, "it's brains, not brawn we need in the Corps. You seem to be lacking in the first department, bud."

Tanner ignored him. "Looks like we got us a feisty one!"

Rowena knew she'd have her work cut out to beat up this creep. "Tell you what, soldier, you know anything about pie-eating?"

Tanner's eyes almost popped out of his head. "Pie eating, I'm the platoon champ for God's sake. Tell me you didn't know!"

"Actually, pal, I didn't know but I'll take you on. Loser cleans the latrines for a week!"

A look of disbelief crossed Tanner's face. He laughed; how could he lose? Then this little runt could work her sweet ass off all week in the toilets!

"OK, OK, settle down peeps!" It was Lieutenant Rushmore. He addressed the dining room in a booming voice. "I heard all that and I'll get Sergeant Shiner to set up the competition. Breakspear, it's your lucky day. You were down for latrine-cleaning duty next week, now it'll be Martens ... or Sutherland, of course," he added hastily. "Also, listen up peeps, we need a candidate from this camp for the National U.S. Army Pie Eating Competition in Atlanta in the Fall. I propose that the winner of this Eat Off be that candidate. Anyone got any objections to that, come and see me afterwards."

Rowena sat gazing out of the train windows as the fields and woods flashed past. In the far distance she could see the first foothills of the Santa Cruz mountains. She was going home. She'd given it her best shot but at the end of the day, the army was all about killing people, no matter how they tried to dress it up. After much soul searching, she'd handed in her dog tags and was heading back to her parents' house. She stroked her belly where new life was beginning.

Her mind flitted back to the contest. The evening of the competition came and Rowena and Tanner sat side by side, with hands tied behind their backs. Rowena had eaten a huge meal eighteen hours earlier, mainly easily-digestible fruit and vegetables, high in fibre. She'd eaten for nearly an hour, then after ten minutes, she'd drunk water until her stomach was at bursting point. After a night punctuated by toilet visits had followed a light breakfast of pancakes and frequent drinks of electrolyte and a protein shake during the day. At 4 p.m. she'd gone for a light two-mile run. Now her stomach was empty again, she was hungry as hell and ready to chow down!

All she remembered after that was the shouting and hollering of a couple of hundred GI's, oblivious to everything apart from the next pie being placed before her and burying her teeth into the crust and apple filling. She never wanted to eat another apple as long as she lived!

Whilst in the rock-climbing club, she'd perfected the art of competitive eating, chewing gum constantly to strengthen her jaws and maxing out on big meals and water to stretch her stomach to the limit, even having her teeth filed to bite through tough fillings more easily. But the army was a harder taskmaster. When the final whistle blew, she'd eaten the fillings and most of the top crust of four and a half pies. The bottom crust was not to be disturbed. Out of the corner of her eye she'd spotted Tanner chomping like a man possessed and tried to put him out of her mind, battling the clock only.

Now, she was dismayed to see he had almost finished his fifth pie. Her heart sank as her hands were freed and she was able to wipe the muck off her face. A week cleaning latrines – shit!

Then she heard Tanner give a large belch and smelt vomit. There it was on his chin. Before he could wipe it off, a huge cheer went up as a judge waved a red flag above Tanner's head. Disqualified for vomiting. Rowena was the platoon pie-eating champ!

However, Rowena was petrified of flying and the army baulked at paying for her time off to travel to Atlanta and back by rail. So, to her dismay, her pie-eating career had ended and Tanner was reinstated as camp eating champion.

She patted her belly. She didn't know or care which of her 'well-wishers' the father was or whether the baby would be black, brown, yellow or white. Nor did she care what her parents would think. The army was history. *This* was her job now. To be the best mother she could be. She brightened up. Anyway, thinking about it, wasn't it nearly time for the rock-climbing club's annual pie-eating contest?

What's in a Name?

Dr. Letitia Scott stood at an enormous round window, gazing in awe at the towering pyramidal blocks a thousand stories high that dominated the city. She never grew tired of looking at them nor ceased to wonder at their immensity. Multi-coloured sky pods darted around and between them. A bleep from her pager jolted her out of her reverie. The director, Dr. Abraham Klein, wished to see her urgently. What the hell did the old bugger want?

She knocked softly and entered the chamber. Klein's office was circular and enormous, and painted in brilliant white. Huge oval windows in the ceiling far above showed a cerulean sky dotted with small white clouds. Dr. Klein did not look happy, she thought.

"Take a seat, Dr. Scott." Klein gestured to a sumptuous white chair and retreated behind his desk. He sat down and rested his chin on the inverted 'V' of his fingertips. "It's about the Oceanic Integrity Committee."

Letitia crossed her legs, admiring her slim calves, trim ankles and painted toe nails. The hours on the treadmill were paying off, much as she disliked the old-fashioned methods. "Yes?"

"It's being headed up by Professor Yasarin."

"What!" Letitia almost exploded. She stood up, put both hands on the edge of the enormous desk and looked Dr. Klein directly in the eyes. "What the hell are you saying?"

Dr. Abraham Klein's eyes wavered, looked down at the polished amboyna burl, then, bracing himself, back into Letitia's. "Look, I knew you wouldn't be happy."

"You can say that again!"

"He's a changed man, into environmental conservation, reforestation, breeding endangered species, stricter emission controls …."

"For Chrissakes. If he'd got his way at the 2030 climate summit, we'd all have drowned in our beds by now!"

"Look, he was wrong, we all know he was wrong; he openly admits he was wrong. Anyone can make a mistake."

"Oh, opposing anyone and everyone who argued for emission controls for ten years. A mistake!"

"Now, now, Dr. Scott, listen to the man. Be reasonable." A smooth voice with a hint of Russian accent came from behind.

Letitia whirled around, surprised. The man had entered the chamber soundlessly.

Professor Yasarin adjusted silver-rimmed glasses on his Roman nose. She had to admit he was quite handsome, in that cruel Gulag-commandant way. She could feel his eyes scanning over her, undressing her mentally. "Dr. Scott, er, Letitia, if I may be so bold. Look, I know we haven't always seen eye to eye."

"Pfft!"

"But, look, things have changed, I myself have changed, and now I want you onboard. Onboard as someone on the committee I can trust to make the right decisions. The right decisions to care for our oceans."

"OK, well, look, they'll come at a price." Letitia looked from Professor Yasarin to Dr. Klein and back to the professor.

The professor took a seat and put his head back, staring at the distant ceiling. "Yes?"

She continued, "One, I get the right of veto, two, I move to the office on the top floor, and three, er, I want the next research vessel named after me."

The professor laughed. "Is that all?" whilst Dr. Klein made a noise like a fart.

Letitia looked down at her holographic nails, watching seagulls fly. "Uh huh."

"Well, my dear, I'll tell you what. Why don't I take you out for dinner and we can discuss it?"

Letitia looked from Klein's apoplectic visage to Professor Yasarin. She noticed his teeth were white and straight, something she always looked for in a lover. "Well, I'm free tonight."

Shelly in the Jungle

"Where d'you think I'm gonna find that kinda money?" asked Shelly Green, pulling on her dog's lead. "Sit, Earl, sit!"

"Listen Shell', it's a chance in a lifetime! I dunno, get a loan from the bank, sell your car, sell your house!"

Shelly sighed. "What about Wharton's. They wouldn't let me go for a month!"

"For Chrissakes, Shelly, you're only a cleaner. They can get someone else from the agency. No offence."

"Thanks a lot!" Shelly blushed. Her friend, Mavis Enderby didn't mince words. "But, look, Mave, those pygmies, with their beards and loincloths and sweaty bodies, I mean, what about ... y'know, women's things ... I'd be embarrassed!"

Mavis deposited her ample backside on a garden chair and took out her laptop. "When in Rome, do as the Romans. You'll get used to jungle life, and I'll be with you, I'm the tour guide, don't forget." She tapped on the keyboard. The flight leaves on the 22nd December. Just think, you'll get to celebrate New Year in the jungles of New Guinea!"

"Oh, yeah, singing *Old Lang Syne* with a bunch of sweaty, spear-waving pygmies – no thank you! Anyway, I've got to take Earl for a walk. Have some more *prosecco*, I'll be back in half an hour."

When Shelly returned, she was shocked to find Mavis had stripped down to her bra and panties, smeared her face and body with soil and was now brandishing a garden cane as if it were a spear. Earl began to bark loudly.

"Shut up!" The dog carried on barking until Shelly slapped his backside. "Hey, that cane was holding my string beans!"

Mavis began to dance around in a circle, jiggling her sizeable bottom and waving her 'spear.' "You white woman, you welcome to our village. You hold pig whilst I club its head!"

"You're mad, Mave, y'know!"

Laughing and breathless, Mavis sat down and threw her 'spear' to the ground.

"Sorry, I got carried away. Maybe the *prosecco* had something to do with it."

Shelly noticed the bottle was empty.

―――

Several months later, older and wiser, Shelly sat in her garden, basking in the summer sun. She'd got over her anger at selling her cherished car to pay for Mavis's 'Christmas Jungle Experience,' arriving in New Guinea to find her friend conspicuous by her absence. Instead, along with a motley crew of oddballs, they'd had to hire their own tour guide, a native by the name of Umberto. Then had followed weeks of hacking through jungle paths and 'toileting' behind trees, keeping a wary eye out for poisonous snakes. She'd lost her job at Wharton's but, hey, she'd got a job on the checkouts at Tesco, which she preferred. Now she'd invited Mavis around to patch things up.

The garden gate opened and in came Mavis, holding a huge bunch of red roses and a vase-shaped package, wrapped in cream paper with red stripes. "Hello, kiddo, how was New Guinea? I'm sorry, kid, I couldn't go, I broke a toe getting out of bed. No hard feelings?"

"No hard feelings, Mave."

"Well, you made it home, anyway. I guess you've got *some* good memories?"

Shelly smiled. "More than memories, actually, Mave. *Umberto!*"

The back door opened and out came a man in bathing trunks. His body was short, but lithe and brown. He sported a bushy black beard and matching curly hair. "Greetings, Mavis, Shelly much tells me about you."

"Oh, all good, I hope," Mavis improvised, taken aback.

"Yes, and we invite you to our wedding."

Mavis recovered, casting an envious glance at Shelly, "How lovely, thank you. Of course I'll come. I promise this time!"

Umberto smiled. "Thank you, dear Mavis. It will be on anniversary of Shelly coming in my country, the 22nd of December. You will be special guest!"

"Oh, thank you."

"And to be held with my tribe in foothills of Papua, New Guinea."

For once, Mavis Enderby was speechless.

Something to Do With the Sea

Credited, usually, with the patience of a saint, I was nevertheless tested at times.

"I'm looking for a book."

I looked up from my desk at the back of the shop, where I was cataloguing a copy of Pepys's diary, bound in worn morocco leather that had no doubt, decades earlier, been an impressive maroon. The man was tall, ascetic, with a boyish face. His black hair was neatly parted and his nose was thin and pronounced. Ominously, he sported a dog-collar.

"Ah, yes, what's it called."

"Oh, that I'm not sure about. It's quite a long title."

"Well, who's it by? I can look it up for you."

"Ah, hmm, the name escapes me right now." He gazed around the shelves intently, as if it were his first venture into a second-hand bookshop.

I felt the first bubblings of annoyance. "Well, look, what's it about. Is it fiction or non-fiction?"

He looked down at me, blinking rapidly. "Oh, it … it's non-fiction. Sorry, I'm not being much help, am I?"

"Well, is it a book on theology?" I suggested helpfully, taking account of his garb.

He smiled. "No, even us rectors need to read something other than the bible!"

"Look, can you remember *anything* about it?"

"Yes, it's blue, and I think … an American author, something to do with the sea."

Oh, that narrowed it down to a couple of million books then. I smiled my best bookshop-owner's smile. "Look, perhaps you could come back when you have the author and title? But, while you're here, why not have a look around. It might jog your memory?"

He returned to the counter some twenty minutes later clutching a number of books, just as I'd moved on to cataloguing a dog-eared copy of *The Collected Letters of Samuel Johnson.* Truth to tell I was glad of the diversion from Mr. Johnson's wordy missives. "Did you find the book?"

"What book?".

"The one you asked me about when you came in!"

"Ah, no, alas, it's gone clean out of my mind. I do hate it when that happens, don't you?"

Well it was part of my job that things *didn't* go 'clean out of my mind' but I concurred politely, totting up books on chess, crosswords, violin-playing and one on how Aristotle invented science, to a respectable thirty-five pounds. That would at least cover heating and lighting for the day, I reflected.

The following morning, the shop bell rang and a woman appeared, her ample figure clothed in black. Her hair was platinum white, cut in a neat bob and she wore a little powder, pale-blue eye shadow and pink lipstick. She carried a book on chess – *Rubinstein's Fifty Best Games*, which I recognised as one I'd sold to the vicar the previous day.

"Can I help?" I asked.

"Yes." She gave a pleasant smile. "My husband bought this yesterday. I'm afraid he's rather absent-minded. He'd already got a copy."

Absent-minded seemed too kind but I smiled back. "I can refund you," I said, ignoring my usual policy. "By the way, did he remember the book he was after."

She handed me a slip of paper on which was written in neat fountain-pen, *The Seven Habits of Highly Effective People. Stephen R Covey.*

Trying to keep a straight face, I said, "Well, you're in luck. I've got a copy in the back. I'll just fetch it."

I returned moments later with a virtually unread copy. The previous owner didn't seem to have scored too high on the effectiveness scale. "You can have it for … er, three pounds."

"Oh, that's wonderful," she exclaimed, taking the book and flicking through it with pink-painted nails. "My name's Susan by the way. My husband – the vicar – is Cecil." She held out her hand.

I shook it and stood mesmerised as her jade-green eyes stared into mine.

She seemed in no hurry to release her grip. "Look, you must come to tea." She proffered a card. "Tomorrow would be good." Glancing at a sign, she said, "How about four o'clock? I see you close early." Hesitating, she added, "Although Cecil will be at choir practice till five, I'm afraid." She didn't *look* too afraid.

"Oh, that'll be OK." I thought I could live without Cecil's company for an hour.

She smiled and handed me three pounds.

In the words of Mr Covey himself, it had all the hallmarks of a win-win situation!

Wounded Walking

"What are you talking about, I don't have a sister!"

Maurice Humphries was taken aback. Surely this gentleman, the last of the group to arrive, was the Reverend Herbert Galton? Apparently to be accompanied by his sister, Dolly. "You *are* Reverend Galton, are you not?"

"I am *Colonel* Galton. Kenneth. The reverend is my brother."

Humphries regarded the motley crew of walkers gathered underneath the old railway bridge at Woodman's Hyde. They stood, shuffling, fiddling with maps and compasses, clad in brightly coloured tops sporting names such as North Face, Berghaus and Patagonia.

The colonel, by contrast, wore a Barbour jacket and high leather boots, looking for all the world as if he were going on a pheasant shoot.

"Oh, I don't have you on the list," Humphries said.

"No matter," snapped the colonel, "you can put me on it now."

Humphries hesitated, his travel-agent training taking over, "Well, um, I'm not sure. There's insurance to be considered—"

"Herbert said it'd be OK."

"Well, um—"

"Oh, here he comes now," said the colonel, as a tall thin man wearing a dog collar approached, accompanied by a woman with a round pink face encircled by a halo of white hair.

"Ah, hello, Ken, good morning, everyone," said the reverend, "sorry we're a bit late. Dolly here couldn't find her dentures."

Dolly's rouged lips parted in a smile, showing a large area that could have been a black hole.

"OK, everyone," Humphries announced loudly, deciding to let the insurance matter go. "As you know, the plan is to walk along the old railway line to Glebe Farm then to take the bridle path to Dunnock's Hill then back here, over the fields, for lunch at the Railway Inn." He gestured to a large white building just visible in the distance through the blackened stone arch that dwarfed the narrow country lane. "I understand they do a very good all-day breakfast, and I can personally recommend the mild, I could drink a gallon of the stuff!"

"Can we go there now?" someone asked. Everyone laughed.

"There won't be any dogs at this farm will there?" asked a frail old man with a walking stick. "It's just that ... well, I'm scared of dogs. Ever since one bit me in the crotch when I was a nipper."

"Why didn't you nip it back then!" laughed Nurse Sandra Bagshot, a comely woman in her forties.

Humphries consulted his map. "Don't worry, Mr Peebles, if there are, they'll already have been fed, and, anyway, you've got your stick to beat them off with."

"Oh, dear, well I don't know if I can beat off a pack of vicious dogs with this." Peebles brandished his stick feebly in the air.

Everyone laughed.

"Come on" said Humphries, leading the way up a steep path to the old track bed.

Two hours later the group sat at adjacent tables in the dining room of the historic Railway Inn, where a roaring fire kept the old room at a claustrophobic temperature. Humphries looked around the dozen in the group, unloading rucksacks and taking off layer after layer of outdoor gear. Surely they were the most incompetent bunch it had ever been his misfortune to lead on a walk? It wasn't as if they'd been going up the north face of the Eiger for heaven's sake!

"Mr Humphries, may I sit next to you?" It was Nurse Sandra Bagshot.

Humphries nodded assent and was mollified by the feeling of her large soft hip against his. He took a pint of mild from a tray and swallowed several mouthfuls, enjoying the silky warm liquid in his mouth and throat, and feeling the room reel slightly, despite the low alcohol. "It was fortuitous, you joining us today, Sandra. Thank you."

She smiled, "Well, I thought I was just coming on a walk. I mean," she whispered conspiratorially, "I thought the reverend and the colonel were going to come to blows, all that sibling rivalry!" She laughed. "And I hadn't expected to give resuscitation," she nodded towards old Arthur Peebles, clad in a blanket and sipping whisky, who smiled weakly in their direction.

Humphries coughed. "How was I to know there'd be a pack of foxhounds at the farm. It was just bad luck."

Dolly tapped him on the shoulder, "Thank you for the nice walk, Mr Humphries, and I'm sorry about your foot. Why I'd wrapped them up in that handkerchief I simply can't imagine." She gave an unbroken pearly smile. "Thank goodness Nurse Bagshot had a first aid kit in her rucksack."

"It was my fault," said Humphries, "if only those damned laces hadn't broken." He took off a boot and rubbed his foot where a denture-shaped cut lay under a bandage. "A highly unfortunate coincidence!"

"I say, Humphries," came the strident voice of the colonel, "what's the next walk you're doing?"

"The Viking Way, two weeks' time. And don't worry, Mr Peebles, there won't be any Vikings!"

He felt the comforting squeeze of Sandra Bagshot's hand on his arm.

"Just rest your foot for a week, won't you, Maurice? It'll soon heal then."

"OK."

Her large blue eyes gazed into his. "And could I get you another drink?"

"Oh, er, yes please. Another pint of mild would be nice." Humphries watched as Nurse Bagshot's fulsome figure headed towards the bar. Well, maybe it hadn't been such a bad day after all!

Tastes Like Hippopotamus to Me

Sprong and Brackett was distinguishable from other shops by the broomsticks, pointed hats and mountain of strange bric-a-brac in its bowed windows. Candles, crystals, and incense sticks rubbed shoulders with figurines of nature spirits, oracle cards and pendants of all shapes and sizes. Marcy pushed the door open and a bell rang. No one was around. She went through to the back and saw a small glass phial on a table. She put it in a pocket and left an envelope in its place. Then she hurriedly exited the shop.

Back at work, Marcy went to the kitchen where several chefs were bustling around and where Fred, the electrician, was tinkering with a fan.

"I don't like the look of these bearings, they could go any day."

Marcy laughed, taking in Fred's good looks and muscular physique. "You always say that, Fred. They're still working. Just learn to relax." She put the phial on the side and sat down to rest her feet for a minute, inhaling the scent of frying garlic. Her mind went back to her previous job, working in a call centre. How she'd hated the job, how rude the customers were and how her superior, Hilda's, body odour made her feel sick. Then, by a stroke of luck, a friend had recommended her to Reubens, one of the most exclusive eating houses in the country. Marcy had met Billy, the owner of the three-Michelin-starred restaurant, and he'd taken a shine to her.

"Is everything all right?" Marcy asked a diner.

"I don't believe this steak is from a zebra," said a large woman with a round, flushed face. "Tastes more like hippopotamus to me."

There was always one, Marcy thought. "I can assure you it is, Madam, the manager shot it himself. It was flown back from Nigeria the next day. If you like, he'll show you photographs of the kill."

The woman seemed to lose interest, "No, that's all right, the two *can* taste similar." She filled her cavernous mouth with a large lump of meat, topped with mashed potato and gravy.

Reubens had been a revelation to Marcy. Reservations had to be made months, even years, in advance. The restaurant boasted an A-Z menu, from aardvark to zebu, and, of course, astronomical prices. She'd wondered why the restaurant had been so popular, even amongst the not-so-rich who saved for months for a meal there. Then, after she'd been waiting on tables for three months, Billy had called her into his office and told her – under oath – the secret. Every meal had a few drops of a love potion added to it. Shortly afterwards, she was put on the rota to collect the daily potion supply from a nearby witchcraft shop, Sprong and Brackett. In case of problems, a few days' worth of potion was kept in a safe.

"Marcy, do you have a moment please." It was Billy Reuben. He looked worried.

She followed him to his office, where a tall man with thinning silver hair, black-framed glasses and a long, pointed nose sat with a pile of ledgers.

"This is Mr. Galton."

Galton gave a cursory nod.

"Look, Marcy, I'm sorry to have to ask this," Billy continued, "but, well, you weren't employed here on account of your brains." He nodded towards her not-inconsiderable chest. "To be honest, we're in the shit. Yes, I know we charge an arm and a leg but all these flights from Africa and the jungles of South Asia don't come cheap, and we're three months behind with the rent."

Galton coughed.

Billy continued, "Well, Mr. Galton has kindly agreed to give us another month to bring the account up to date if you would, well, er, not to beat around the bush, er … spend the night with him."

Marcy felt her face flush. Well, she knew she was 'eye-candy' but, even so! She pulled a face. "I don't know."

Just then, the door burst open and Fred, the electrician, came in, singing and dancing, his face red and his eyes shining. "Ooh,

I feel love, I feel love." He gyrated his hips, then made a bee line for Galton, who had risen to his feet, astonished. Fred hugged him and kissed him full on the lips. Fred looked at Marcy and laughed, "I don't know what happened, I took a little swig from that bottle you left on the side – it smelled so nice, and it tasted so good I just had to drink it all. Now I just love *everyone*!"

Marcy cringed at her forgetfulness.

Galton eyed Fred up and down. "Actually, I swing both ways. This chap'll do."

They left hand-in-hand as Billy smiled and poured himself and Marcy a glass of extremely expensive champagne.

Here's Looking at Your Kid

"Well, did you hear about Gary?" Nadine's face was flushed, as if drunk.

"No."

"He's just beaten the telesales record for the whole year and he's only been here a month!"

It was July. "What?!"

"Well, Malcolm just posted the sales on the board. Go and look!" She laughed. "Speak of the Devil!"

Gary appeared, grinning from ear to ear. He was a 'ginger,' and sported a neat beard. A fan of Prince Harry perhaps? "It's true folks, I'm the number one salesman, sorry, sales *person*!"

"What's your secret, Gary?" I asked, feeling a little shy, now he'd proven himself to be such a potent newcomer.

He looked directly into my eyes and I noticed his, a pale blue, like the birds' eggs me and my brother would take from nests, still warm, when we were kids. They opened wide. "Well Flora, the trick is to stop them hanging up. I'll try a few angles, quickly, see if I can find out what makes them tick." His translucent blue eyes bored into mine. I couldn't look away. "Like you, Flora, what's your number one interest?"

I spoke from the heart. "Well, my twins. I just want them to do well at school. Get good results, not be bullied, that kinda thing."

"So, you'd be interested in software that'd help with their studies, of course?" The blue eyes continued to gaze into mine.

I felt light-headed. "Yes, if it covers the National Curriculum, I suppose I would."

I looked down at a pink software sales slip. Seemed I'd signed up for *Maths for Movers!* and *English for Champs!* "Where's Gary?" I asked Nadine.

"He just went. Are you OK?" She sounded concerned.

"Yes, sorry, my mind's gone blank. One minute I was talking to Gary, then ...."

"Who was Pythag ... Pythagoronous?" asked Andrew, aged ten.

"Pythagoras! He discovered the rule about the square on the hypotenuse, what you were supposed to have been watching! Weren't you paying attention?"

"Yes, it was saying something about his followers. Did they have Facebook then?"

"Don't be silly, this was over two thousand years ago! Those were the Pythagoreans, they followed his teachings. Some of his ideas were accepted and some weren't. They're still going."

"Huh?"

"Also, Pythagoras invented the musical scale. There, bet you didn't know that!"

"I'm hungry!"

"Didn't Kathy call you for tea?"

"No, she's in a bad mood. Something to do with her boyfriend."

Bloody Kathy! We'd hired her to work in our kitchens four days a week – we ran a small cafe, adjoining the house. She was supposed to fix the kids' lunch and tea too, but recently she seemed to spend more time arguing on the phone with her new boyfriend than working. I'd have to have a word with her. My stomach felt queasy at the thought. I wasn't one for showdowns. "Where's Ally?"

"Watching that English software you gave us."

Just then Kathy came into the lounge.

No time like the present! "Look Kathy, er, we need to speak …."

"If it's about John, it's all over. I've found out he's a …." She looked at Andrew. "Well, not to mince words, a pervert!"

"What?!"

"He's a smooth-talking conman, sells software for school kids that comes with a free virus! It lets paedophiles control kids' webcams and send them instant messages!"

I had a sudden thought. "This, 'John.' He doesn't have ginger hair and a beard by any chance."

Kathy's jaw dropped. "How on earth …?!"

Allison, Andrew's twin came into the room, naked from the waist up, save for her 'training' bra.

"Oh my God, did you just get a message to strip off?" I exclaimed.

Allison looked horrified. "What are you on about, mum?"

"There might have been a pervert using your computer to spy on you!"

Oh, what?! I spilt coffee on my top, I was just going for a clean one. Anyway, *I* should be so lucky!"

Stone the Crows

"'Course, it might have been a false one, to throw us off the scent," said the constable.

"Maybe. These bastards are clever ... Hi, who's that?" said the inspector.

A dark blue Range Rover had just pulled into the car park at Strubby House. A woman in a red coat and matching hat got out, waving. "Cooee."

Thirty minutes earlier, the two policemen, accompanied by a police artist, had taken the path from Strubby House to the Dower House. The latter was a square Georgian pile with tall, narrow windows. Against the gloom of the sinking winter sun it looked like an enormous tomb.

The path, an uneven gravel walkway, strewn with wet leaves, was lined by heavily pollarded beech trees on either side. Their stunted, blackened branches reminded the inspector of photographs of Holocaust victims, dumped in mass graves.

A crow landed on a branch, somewhere just behind them, and began to caw loudly, to the inspector's annoyance. He had an inexplicable hatred of crows.

The policemen reached the front door, the constable knocking on an ancient brass knocker. A footman, dressed in a maroon gown, opened the door. He gestured extravagantly. "Come in gentlemen, her ladyship is expecting you."

They proceeded through to a large lounge filled with antique furniture, where a thin, bird-like woman, whose head was surrounded by a halo of wild, white hair, sat on a chaise-longue. "Would you gentlemen like tea?" she enquired.

"No, we're on a tight schedule. Thank you," said the inspector.

"That'll be all, Pycroft. Please be seated, gentlemen."

The inspector wasted no time on formalities. "Your son, Lord Strubby, said you saw a green *Fiesta* close to the HSBC bank in Cloughtonby yesterday, and that you observed the driver, looking anxious, apparently waiting for someone, Is that correct?"

"Yes, inspector."

"I can confirm that we believe it to have been the getaway vehicle."

"I see."

"As you may have heard, a bank employee was shot in the face and is currently on life support."

"Oh dear." She cocked her bird-like head to one side.

"He may pull through, although he'll have no face left … to speak of, anyway," added the constable, helpfully.

The inspector continued, gesturing to his other companion. "This gentleman, Mr. Thorpe, is a police artist. We'd like to get a rough sketch today, then a proper e-fit at the station tomorrow. Is that OK?"

The woman gave a quick nodding motion of the head, like a chicken pecking in the dirt.

The artist began. "Now, was he black or white?"

"Yellow."

"Yellow?"

"Yes, Chinese I believe."

Mr Thorpe chewed the end of a pencil. "I see. Did he have any distinguishing marks?"

"Well, yes, he did. He had a small tattoo of a dragon on his neck, just here." She indicated a patch just below her right ear, visible through the wispy white mop. "Oh, and he had a scar on his left cheek …." She drew a bony finger from the bridge of her pointed nose across her pale cheek, almost to her earlobe.

Twenty minutes later they left, the inspector well pleased with the sketch produced by Mr. Thorpe. It should just make the seven o'clock news.

They made their way back up the path in the half-light. The crow was still there, a squat black shape. To the inspector's annoyance, on seeing them, it began to caw again.

Now, the woman in the red coat approached. "I do apologise, Inspector, I was held up at a meeting. I hope Pycroft looked after you?"

The inspector looked bemused. "Sorry Madam, and who are you?"

"Oh, I'm Lady Strubby."

"What? Who was the lady in the Dower House we just interviewed then?"

"Oh, dear. Er, that's my sister, ... I'm afraid she's, well, to put it bluntly ... insane. I'm afraid Pycroft *will* humour her."

"But *you* can give us a description, then?" asked the inspector, employing all the restraint he could muster.

"No, I'm terribly sorry. I'm afraid there was a mix up. When my son said it was a green *Fiesta* you were looking for, I misheard him. I thought he said it was *grey*. That was the one I saw. Definitely grey."

The crow alighted on a nearby tree and began to caw loudly again.

The inspector gritted his teeth. "Oh, that'll be all then, thank you, your ladyship."

"Very well, then. Good day." Lady Strubby turned and made her way to the house, shortly disappearing behind a high box hedge.

"Shall we go, sir?" asked the constable.

"Yes, you two go on ahead. I'll join you in a minute."

As Mr. Thorpe and the constable proceeded to the car park, the inspector looked around furtively, then, glancing at the still-cawing crow, bent down to pick up a handful of gravel.

The Name is Grey

"Cloak and dagger man?" asked Clunch.

"My name is Grey, Parma Grey," I replied, "like a mouse's back, and I have a cloak, incarnadine in hue, but, alas, no dagger."

He gave that queer, lopsided grin of his. "Ah, Mr. Grey, immortalised throughout our fair islands. Do come in."

I followed Clunch into a blue pavilion. The Ministry of Covert Warfare's idea of keeping a low profile. "Hardly immortalized, I'm supposed to be a secret agent!"

Clunch gave a throat-clearing splutter as he pressed a lift button. "Ah, but immortalized amongst we secret people, the cognoscenti of the garotte and poisoned umbrella!"

I tried to suppress a smug smile as the lift proceeded downwards.

The door opened onto a long corridor and we entered the first room on our left, where I was to be given a briefing on my mission. A huge bald man sat in a huge chair behind a huge desk. His name, appropriately, was Hugo. Hugo Mann.

"Mr. Clunch, please bring Mr. Grey the latest assortment of, er, gadgets."

Things had moved on since the days of Aston Martin ejector seats and boats that could take off and fly. Now it was all microelectronics, miniature cameras and bio-weapons. But there was still time for what I called 'fun things.' Umbrellas that could blow a hole in someone and phones that could burn people's hands off.

So, I was shown a range of new gadgets, amongst which I rather took a fancy to a laser pen. Innocuous-looking but with enough power to fry an enemy's eyeballs. "Be sure to keep the safety catch in the 'on' position," exhorted Clunch. Then there was what appeared to be an ammonite, an ancient fossil in two halves, but which had been impregnated with a special kind of plutonium. "Quite harmless," said Clunch, "but put the two halves together for sixty seconds and … well, you'll need a fast car to get out of range!"

"You mean …?"

"Yes."

Finally, clutching a briefcase with enough firepower to start – and finish – a small war, I found myself seated and facing the enormous Mr. Mann again. Surely there was some diet he could go on, I thought.

"No there isn't," he said, as if having read my mind. "It's a genetic thing."

Genetic thing my arse. I'd bet he liked his doughnuts soaked in double cream.

He laughed. "And brandy. Well, Parma," he said, jabbing a finger in my direction, "your mission is to wipe out the Taliban."

"With pleasure," I exclaimed, "the uneducated swine!"

"You'll be parachuting into Kabul tomorrow morning."

"Couldn't I just go by passenger plane, y'know, incognito?"

Mr. Hugo Mann's expansive pink face took on a shiny, sweaty hue. "Hmm. That'd mean getting you a ticket."

"Blimey. Surely the Ministry could manage that!"

"Well, er, I suppose so, if you really don't want to parachute."

"Um, I'd rather not," I said. "You know, there are a lot of insects floating around up above the desert. I don't fancy a mouthful of flying earwig."

He stood up, with difficulty, and reached out a huge sweaty paw. "Good luck, Parma, the country, and indeed the world, is depending on you!"

I shook his hand and surreptitiously wiped the grease off on a handkerchief. "Lead on, Mr. Clunch," I cried, "Afghanistan here I come!"

The Old Fuse Trick

Martha came back from the ladies' loo, grinning like a Cheshire cat. "Julie, you'll never believe who's in the Gin Room!"

"Who?"

"That actor, what's his name, you know, the one who looks like Tom Hanks."

I racked my brains. "Oh, you mean the one who was in that film, oh, what was it called? About the air force, you know."

"Yeah, that's the one. Ooh, he's so dishy."

I took a sip of my vodka and lemon. "Actually, I don't care for him." I put my glass down. "I always think Vodka smells like cement glue, don't you? You know, that stuff boys use to glue kits together."

We were seated in the bar of the Priory Hotel, a quaint old place that comprised a network of small rooms, variously used for dining or just sitting, drinking and staring at ancient photographs on the walls. The Gin room was so called as there were numerous empty gin bottles on shelves that covered two walls, the rest of the space being taken up by old books. I supposed the bottles were of renowned gins, if there were such things, otherwise why display them?

The manager, Saul, appeared, a large fellow with black collar-length hair and a beard. He smiled. "Good evening, Julie, good evening, Martha."

"Hi Saul," I said. We were regulars and had often spoken with him.

"Listen, we've a rather famous visitor staying with us."

"Yes, I just saw him," said Martha, "isn't it thrilling!"

"Well, we've a camera crew arriving soon, they're doing a documentary about him."

Martha laughed. "How lovely, I've always wanted to be on TV!"

Saul looked embarrassed. "Sorry, Martha, they don't want anyone else around."

I felt indignant. "What, we've only been here five minutes. Why should we have to push off cos of some ham actor?"

Saul dangled a key in front of us. "If you'd like to go up to this room a waiter will bring you more drinks, and they'll be on the house. We'll call you to let you know when the coast is clear."

Martha seemed to forget about the great actor. "Free drinks! OK, where's this room?"

The room had a four-poster bed and two sofas. A huge arched window looked out over lawns and, just below us, a pond covered with small green lily pads. It was a warm spring evening and I opened a pane, letting in the smell of fresh mown grass and the sound of birds singing.

I laughed. "This is a bit of alright," throwing myself down on the bed. The mattress was deep and enveloped me with its warmth. "Phone down and order us a bottle of chardonnay, hun. Maybe I'll have a kip afterwards!"

"In a minute, I'm just going to the bathroom."

There was a quiet knock on the door. I got up and opened it to a young girl, dressed in black, pulling a vacuum cleaner. She looked apologetic. "Sorry, I've got to clean this room."

"What! Can't you do it later, after whatshisname's buggered off?"

The girl's face flushed. "Sorry, we've had a late booking. It's a doctor who's very anxious that the room be spotless. He's said he'll be here in two hours."

Martha appeared. "Look, tell you what, leave the vacuum cleaner with us and we'll clean the room after we've had a drink." Martha winked at me.

The girl looked down at her feet. "I don't know. He's very fussy."

"Look, don't worry, I used to clean at my dad's hotel." She winked at me again. "You go and take a break. Tell you what, come back in an hour and you can check it's clean enough."

Mollified, the girl left.

"What was that about?" I asked

"Look, we'll do the old fuse trick, that'll knacker the vacuum cleaner, then we can't be blamed for not cleaning the room can we?"

I looked out of a window to see a large van parked up on the narrow pavement and enormous quantities of gear in black wooden crates and aluminium flight cases being unloaded and brought into the hotel.

Suddenly there was a flash of flame and a loud bang. The wall socket where Martha had plugged the cleaner in for her 'trick' was covered in soot.

I flicked a light switch to check they were still working. They weren't.

"Whoops," said Martha.

Shortly, there came another, louder, knock on the door. It was Saul, red-faced and agitated. He looked at the sooty wall socket. "What on earth's going on? All the electrics have gone, in the rooms, in the kitchen. The fuse board's up the creek. I've called an electrician. He reckons half an hour to get here and sort it out."

"I don't know," said Martha, "The vacuum cleaner must have short-circuited."

"What were you doing with the vacuum cleaner, for heaven's sake?"

"Oh, I just fancied a spot of cleaning. I can't help myself. Can we go down to the bar then?"

Saul looked like he was about to explode.

Just then, a famous face appeared at the door. "Excuse me, I hope you ladies won't mind but I want to keep out of the way of autograph hunters while they're sorting the electrics out. Would you mind if I join you? Saul, could you bring us a bottle of your best champagne, please?"

Martha looked at me, wide-eyed. Her face was flushed and her lips opened soundlessly. She looked like she was going to pass out.

"Yeah, that'll be OK, take a pew," I said, patting the unoccupied cushion next to me on the sofa. "My name's Julie, but you can call me Juju."

There Was None Bolder

"Calm down now and listen up," said our sixth form tutor, Miss Hughes. "That includes you, Kara Simons." She jabbed a finger in my direction. "Now, today's the first of our career sessions and I'm pleased to welcome our two guests to speak about their careers and what you could expect if you were to follow in their footsteps."

I looked from a twenty-something woman in a pink two-piece to a man of a similar age, clad in camouflage get-up, olive green with grey-white bits. He wore a green beret with two rows of little white and red squares at the bottom, and a thick black belt. His lips were thin and he looked around the classroom with disdain.

"This is Miss Cheskin," said Miss Hughes, gesticulating to the woman. "She's here to talk about a career in retail sales."

The woman stepped to the front and gave a bright smile. "So, how many of you like the idea of working in a department store? Hands up."

A plain spotty girl, Ruth Smith, lifted a fat arm up. "Wouldn't mind."

"I wouldn't want to be served by you!" said Johnny Harris. The class laughed.

"That's enough, Harris," snapped Miss Hughes. "Please carry on, Miss Cheskin."

Miss Cheskin carried on, "Well, I've been employed by John Lewis for almost ten years …." She proceeded to tell us story after boring story of serving on the women's accessory department, drawing floor layouts on the blackboard accordingly.

I looked around and winked at Tom Jarvis. He winked back, rolling his eyes to the ceiling. I had to say I quite fancied Tom. I tore a piece of notepad off as quietly as I could, pleased that Miss Hughes didn't look my way. I drew a heart with an arrow through it, writing the initials KS and TJ on either side, folded it up and passed it to Nora Evans, sitting next to me, jerking my head in Tom's direction. "Pass it on," I mouthed.

"And it's most important to keep an accurate inventory of stock," Miss Cheskin said to the glazed eyes of the class. Thankfully, it seemed there were no further anecdotes and that was the end of her talk. She smiled. "So, I hope that's given you some idea of the fun you can have if you work for John Lewis!"

The corpulent Ruth Smith began to clap, then realising no one else was following her lead, her claps grew slower and softer and she turned beetroot red.

"Thank you so much, Miss Cheskin, that was most interesting. Now I'd like to present Lance Corporal Lachlan McGlothlin," said Miss Hughes.

The class sat up as the soldier marched to the front of the class, grim-faced, thin-lipped and with a nose that looked like it had seen a fair few boxing matches. His small black eyes bore around the class like a laser beam. *"Dae ony o' ye lads wantae jyne th' airmie then,"* he announced with a broad Scottish accent.

"Do any of you boys want to join the army?" translated Miss Hughes.

Ruth Smith put her fat arm up once more. "Wouldn't mind."

"Noo listen lassy th' army's na steid fur th' likes o' ye," snapped the Lance Corporal, no translation being needed.

Tom Jarvis put his hand up. "I'd be interested, sir."

Just then, my note was surreptitiously handed to Tom. But not surreptitiously enough for the Lance Corporal. *"Whit's that laddie?"* he demanded, marching over and snatching it from Tom's hand. A semblance of a smile broke over the soldier's brutish face. *"Och sae ye'v git a sweet hert in th' class."*

Tom looked around blankly. "What me, no."

The Lance Corporal screwed my note up and hurled it to land right in the centre of the waste paper bin to a round of applause. His thin lips turned up slightly in acknowledgement. *"Listen, in th' airmie, ye hae tae hae dominion ower th' enemy, tis aboot killing fowk at th' end o' th' day!"*

Just then I noticed that the clock must have stopped. It only showed ten minutes of the period had gone but old Miss Department Store must have been yakking and sketching for half an hour. Miss Hughes noticed it too. "Oh, the clock's stopped, does anyone have the time."

"Quarter to, Miss," said Herbert Braddock, the class creep.

"Oh dear, I'll have to get the caretaker to look at it."

"Och let me hae a quick keek," said the soldier marching round Miss Hughes' desk and reaching up to fiddle with the clock fixings. *"A've some batteries oan me."*

Then the strangest thing happened. The Lance Corporal froze, his face turned pale and he began to step backwards. Above the clock face we now observed the long hairy legs of a huge black spider. The soldier began to visibly sway.

"Don't worry," laughed Miss Cheskin, "it's only a spider, a *Tegenaria Parietina*, I believe, probably a boy. We get them in the store rooms. According to the experts, they're quite harmless." She grabbed a chair and stood on it, then to gasps from the class put her hand over the spider and closed it to a small fist. She got down and held her fist out towards the Lance Corporal, smiling.

"Och, a'm feart o' spiders," he said in a tremulous voice, then he began to sag and was helped back to his seat by Miss Hughes as Miss Cheskin deposited the spider out of the window.

And that was the end of our first careers talk. Grinning and winking at each other, we left Lachlan McGlothlin, muttering *"Dae ye hae ony enrichments?"* to the fussing of Miss Hughes and Miss Cheskin.

Tom came over. "Hey, Kara, did you send me that note?"

"What if I did?"

"Well, d'you fancy coming out for a Big Mac tonight?"

My blood began to pound. "Maybe. I'll have to check my diary."

Tom smiled and winked. "See you there at seven!"

Letters from Reuben

Papers, papers, papers. Help, I'm drowning in a sea of papers! I really *must* do something about it!

Following advice from a critical but well-meaning friend, I make up a dozen archive boxes and number them with a large chisel-nibbed marker pen. OK, I can now identify a box at twenty paces.

I start to go around my apartment, dumping papers and associated junk unceremoniously into the boxes. Box one, a stack of writing magazines that have been cluttering my desk for months. Why don't I read them? Or write, for that matter? Oh, I don't have time, of course. Well I guess I *could* quit watching endless re-runs of *Seinfeld*, but, well, I wouldn't want to break the habit of a lifetime. Anyway, out of sight, out of mind!

Into box two goes the rubbish off my kitchen table, 'to do' lists, piles of receipts – why don't I just throw them? Oh, I know, I want to get the points put on my loyalty card. Except that I don't have one. So, they're sitting there waiting for me to go back to the supermarket, queue at the customer service desk, ask for an application form, send it off, *then* phone to have the points retrospectively added. All for a few measly bucks. Into the box! I can throw them out when the allowed time has expired, barring the miracle of me actually getting one of their goddamned cards. In the meantime, I don't have to feel guilty.

Box three is stuff off the top of my filing cabinet, piles of unopened letters and bank statements. Why don't I request paperless statements? Well, do you know *anyone* who's had a computer *not* blow a resistor or whatever? Exactly! Then, how do you access your statements? You're stuffed. Like a piglet in a chestnut factory.

The phone rings. "Hello? ... yes, I'm doing it right now, Shelina! Whaddya mean, voice recorder, card index file! ... look, I'm going to the ballet with my mother tonight, I haven't got time for anything like that ... look sorry, I gotta go, hun, speak to you later!"

I open a draw and the contents go into box number four. Letters from Reuben. I'm not brave enough to put them in the shredder. But I didn't see a future for us. Call me weird but I didn't like the things he asked me to do. I didn't like the taste or the smell. Of those blue cheese and sauerkraut pretzels he was always eating, I mean.

Then there's something else in that draw that goes into box number four too. Something I won't mention here but something that makes me go "oooooOOOOOHHHH!!" But, well, I'm a spiritual girl now and I don't like the idea of angels and spirit guides and what have you, seeing me do 'that.' I can live without it. Well, for a week or two. Maybe. We'll see.

My computer beeps. A friend from over the pond, a crummy little country, but, hey, they've got stuff we haven't. Congratulating themselves over their queen and beef heaters and the Beatles. And, they invented football too, though a weird kind where you can't pick the ball up! I'll reply tomorrow. Like I say, I've gotta meet mom soon and those tickets weren't cheap!

Into box number six I throw stuff from my dressing table and bedside cabinet, I've got more makeup than Emmett Kelly, for Chrissakes!

Finally, I gaze in awe at two neat stacks of six boxes, discretely tucked away in a corner. Maybe I could make up another three or four boxes? I look out of the window, down onto apartments below and feel a glow of pride. I'll bet theirs are all cluttered, not like mine!

The phone goes again. "Hi Mom, yes, I'm just about to have a quick shower and get ready … yeah, I'm excited, really looking forward to it … yeah, of course I've got the ticket! … it's right here … well, it *was* right here … hold on."

My eyes flick from the empty surfaces to the pile of boxes and I feel a sick feeling in my stomach. "You say you're picking me up in thirty minutes, Mom?"

Free Money

"Arabic garlic sauce, otherwise known as *thoom*. Freshly made." Vernon Crowther held out a small glass bowl filled with something resembling a whiter version of mayonnaise.

"It looks nice, sir," said Jake Smeddlehurst. He was about twenty, tall and thin, with a pronounced jawline and black hair that flopped over his narrow face and passed his collar. His eyes were dark and sunken. They darted around furtively, avoiding the speaker.

Vernon placed the bowl onto an occasional table, went back into the kitchen, removed his green and white striped apron and emerged, carrying a plate of vegetable slivers and *Doritos*. "Take a seat, Smeddlehurst."

Jake sat down, pushing his hair off his face.

"Try some."

Jake self-consciously dipped a slice of carrot into the *thoom* before crunching down on it. "Mmm, it's delicious, sir!"

"Good! Now, Smeddlehurst, I want you to listen. You carry on, enjoy some more dip." Vernon took a seat in a sumptuous olive-green leather arm chair. "Now, I'm going to be frank with you. I've seen you at work, heard things about you, and, to be truthful, it seems to me you don't have banking in your blood. Am I right?"

Jake quickly swallowed a thoom-coated mushroom. "Well, sir, I play the drums, that's what I really want to do."

"Look, Smeddlehurst, I've been at Halliwell's for nigh on forty years. They've been good to me, but what with Sandra's boating and Wendy's maintenance, not to mention the children's private schools, well ...." His aged face coloured. "The truth is, it's become a nightmare. They've taken me off futures and put me on credit assessment, stuff a monkey could do!"

Jake munched on a piece of courgette, nonplussed.

Vernon continued, "I think we could both do with a substantial cash injection. Am I right?"

Jake took a Dorito, scooped up a giant blob of dip, and pushed it into his mouth. He nodded enthusiastically. "Mmm."

Vernon ceremoniously plonked down a silver-coloured plastic bank card.

"What's that, sir?"

"This is an ATM master card, our service guys use it. This one's been specially modified. Type in a PIN, and you can withdraw any amount, there's no limit!"

Jake's interest suddenly increased tenfold.

"Now, I've got a printout of our top hundred accounts. Some rich bastards have got a fortune!"

"Sir?"

"Well, they're the ones least likely to notice a, shall we say, *spurious* cash withdrawal."

Jake stared. The penny began to drop. "But … er, you wouldn't know the PIN."

Vernon smiled, producing a computer printout. On it were numerals one to a hundred. These were followed by two numbers. One very long one, preceded by a pound sign, and another, just four digits long.

For once Jake's eyes fastened on the speaker. "You mean …."

"Exactly, Smeddlehurst! Go to any hole-in-the-wall machine, pop the card in, type in a PIN, and make an appropriate withdrawal. Say, five thousand. Late Saturday night, early Sunday morning's a good time. Just once a week, or we could be in deep doo doos."

Jake pushed the empty glass dish back and belched. "Oops, pardon, sir."

Vernon reeled from the waft of garlic. "Granted."

"Er, but that'd be illegal, sir!"

Vernon smiled. "Look, I was useful around the tubs myself when I was young. Good cymbals don't come cheap, and now you've got these new-fangled double bass pedals, all shiny titanium!"

Jake's dark eyes became less dark.

"All you need to do is wear a woollen hat over your head and something to obscure your face, or a crash helmet's a good idea. And wear gloves too. You put half the cash in a bag for me and

I'll tell you where to leave it. Best not use the same ATM or account twice. How does that sound?"

"It sounds good, sir, there's just one thing."

"Yes, Smeddlehurst?"

"Is there any more of that dip please?"

In Memoriam

We all know how much we depend on our postmen and postwomen," intoned Arthur, the vicar, concluding the eulogy, "and Barney was one of the best. Everyone loved Barney."

I looked around the packed church. There was Mavis McLung with her cheeky face surrounded by a mop of ginger curls, courtesy of L'Oréal. Then there was Carol Hardaker, her pug-like visage glaring around at the other villagers lining the pews, her bitchiness silenced through necessity for the time being. In the front row sat Maureen, Barney's widow, dressed in a neat black two-piece with a black hat and veil. Her two teenage sons sat to her right, their eyes red and swollen.

My wife, Sue, took my arm as we finally traipsed out into the graveyard and the warm sun of an early spring morning. "What a bunch of hypocrites," she whispered.

"What do you mean?" I asked.

"Well, no one was that bothered about him when he was alive, were they? Sure, they'd say 'Good morning, Barney, and goodbye, Barney,' but be bitching about the post being late behind his back."

"Well, I liked the chap," I said. "Well, I didn't really know him, I suppose, but, well, all those years his little red van would come down our road, come rain or snow."

"Or sun," said Sue. "Well, I spoke to Maureen at Bingo sometimes. She'd talk about all the big houses and farms he'd drive out to, places almost no one knew existed. I always felt she was holding something back though."

"How d'you mean?"

Sue beckoned me away from the rows of mourners screening us from the grave, where the vicar was doing his 'dust to dust' routine, surrounded by Barney's tearful relatives. "Well, I mean, as a postman he'd be privy to a lot of secrets, wouldn't he?"

"Well, like what?"

"Come on, dear, like who was getting summonses, speeding fines, warnings for debt, all that kind of thing. Easy enough to tell from the envelopes, especially if it's your job."

"Hmm. I suppose so." I thought back with embarrassment about the speeding fines I'd had. But didn't everyone get those? Apparently not, according to Sue.

"Then, there's stuff you can feel through the packages, isn't there?"

"Huh?"

"Well, like …," she lowered her voice even further …. "well, like sex toys, y'know, vibrators, dildos that kinda thing."

I felt indignant. "Surely the postmen, er, and women, would be discreet? It'd be more than their jobs would be worth to be seen having a good feel of customers' mail, I'd have thought."

Sue snorted. "Dream on. Oh, look out."

Maureen was coming towards us, flanked by her two sons. We made apologetic noises as she passed.

"And then he'd likely come across people in inappropriate places."

I raised my eyebrows. "Well, like where?"

"Like people shagging other people's wives … or husbands, for instance."

"All in all, sounds like some may have been pleased to see the back of him," I remarked. "Anyway, you go on to the village hall and get us a table. I just want a quick word with, er, Bill Dikkers. About the compost club."

"Blimey, you look like you've just seen a ghost," Sue exclaimed, as I sat down at a table with her, clutching a cup of tea and a cream scone.

"Oh, I just had, er, one of my turns."

"What are you on about, you don't have 'turns.'"

"I was speaking figuratively." I sipped hot weak tea. In fact, I *had* seen a ghost. The ghost of Barney, leaning nonchalantly against the church masonry and puffing on a cigarette. One of the advantages of being a spirit, I surmised. You could hardly die of lung cancer, after all.

He'd been kind of transparent and it seemed I was the only one around who could see him. He'd wagged a finger at me and held up a little black pocketbook. Then he winked and rubbed the first and second fingers of his right hand against his thumb.

Pay up or Maureen would spill the beans seemed to be the message. Plus, I'd be haunted into the bargain, I supposed.

Looking around the room, I noticed a few other faces that might be considered pale and worried. Even Rosie Bale, the sumptuous doctor's wife looked a little off colour. Now, that was a turn up for the books. Either way, it seemed Barney's ghost had been busy.

In a corner, Maureen sat with her sons, chomping on a large ham and cheese sandwich. She caught my eye and gave me what looked like a wink. She was on track to profit from Barney's little 'sideline' for some time to come, I imagined. I decided it might be prudent to continue the payments. After all, fake or not, I never could resist ginger curls.

Postcard from Hispaniola

Hello Darling, well they were right when they said the recipe for a great marriage is to live in different countries! Missing you and 'the babe' though. Looking forward to our 'meeting' in the Autumn! As the pic shows, I'm in Port-au-Prince. Splashed out on a Caribbean Cruise, don't be cross! Someone said, 'You can live to be a hundred, if you give up all the things that make you want to live to be a hundred!' At this rate I'll be dead at sixty! Still, my heart is true to you, never fear! Trust it's still the same with you? Haiti's crazy, a place where a black cat at a crossroads stops everyone, but a red light doesn't! How are the shows going, you don't phone or message me? All that practice that used to drive me nuts finally paid off. You show 'em girl! Tarquin xxxx

Just One Little Crumb

Little Oswald Cobley was heading home through the woods from his school in the village of Ballykenny. He whistled happily and swung his school bag, looking forward to telling his mother how he and his classmates had formed a 'band' in the music lesson, playing on pots and pans from the kitchens, whilst their teacher, Mr. Dumderry, had accompanied them on the bagpipes, to the squawking of the school parrot, Spike.

Suddenly, he was startled by the appearance of an old lady dressed in black. She had a long beaky nose with a conspicuous wart on the end and several long hairs growing from her chin. She held a plate containing a cake and gave a smile, showing two large gaps among her crooked teeth. "Hello, young man, I expect you're hungry after a long day at school. Try a piece of my cake, freshly baked today!"

Oswald remembered his mother's advice. "Never accept food from strangers."

"Why not mother?" he'd asked.

"Well, if you buy it from Mr. Barmwell, the baker, you know he will have checked the ingredients and made sure they were all tip-top and wholesome. If you buy food from a shop, well they have important people who will have made sure the food is healthy and safe to eat."

"Yes, mother."

"But a stranger, well, they could have put poison in it, or worse!"

Oswald scratched his head. "What's worse than poison!"

"Ah, well, there are potions that would turn you into a giant cockroach, or make your arms shrink to nothing, or turn everything you say into a scream of pain, or ...."

"No, I won't mother," Oswald interrupted hastily, not wishing to hear further horrors.

But now the wicked witch, for such was she, held out a crumb from the most delicious-looking cake Oswald had ever seen.

"My mother said I mustn't accept food from strangers."

"Ah, one little crumb can't do any harm, surely?"

Oswald, hesitated, then took the crumb from the old woman's wrinkled hand and popped it into his mouth. "Mmm. This is gorgeous!"

"Here, have some more, young sir." The witch handed over a slice which Oswald snatched from her hand, quickly stuffing as much of it into his mouth as he could.

The following morning, Oswald's mother let out a scream when she went to wake her son. For sticking out some distance beyond the bottom of the bed were Oswald's feet!

"What's the matter, mother?" cried Oswald, springing out of bed and knocking his head on the ceiling.

"Oh, my son, you have turned into a giant in the night! Did you take food from a stranger?"

Oswald looked down on his mother, feeling sheepish. "Just a slice of cake, mother. A very delicious cake!" His mouth watered at the memory.

"Wait, I will fetch the priest, he will know what to do!"

But the priest didn't know what to do and after a few days Oswald was as tall as his parent's house. He could no longer go to school or read books so the teachers rigged up a projector and a giant screen on which they projected his homework.

But Oswald grew and grew. Soon he was the height of two houses, then three houses, then four.

To eat, Oswald had to lie down in the meadow and large quantities of cooked food were dropped into his mouth by helicopter. But before long, he couldn't lie in the meadow without crushing nearby houses with his enormous feet. He could no longer wear shoes or normal clothes, just a robe made from huge sheets.

So, he would feel cold and this made him angry. He would stamp around, crushing cars and buildings with his bare feet, and shouting so loudly it would burst people's eardrums.

"What shall we do, sir?" The Head of the Army asked the Prime Minister.

"Well, I'm sorry to say, Oswald has become a menace. Even when he's in a good mood he's accidentally squashing people and knocking buildings down. There aren't many places left in England where he can go without destroying things."

"Well, how about sending him to Scotland, sir?"

"Yes, that would be good, there are miles and miles of moors and mountains and it wouldn't matter if he crushed a few sheep with those gigantic feet."

But getting him there was the problem. Oswald had grown to the size of a small skyscraper and a fleet of helicopters was now required to bring cooked animal carcasses, truckloads of vegetables and barrels of water to his mouth.

However, Oswald had other ideas. He had grown and grown until, at the age of eight, and a height of half a mile, he was the tallest, naughtiest, and most destructive child in the world – and then some!

Although gigantic, he still had a child's sense of humour, so took pleasure in squatting and depositing steaming, smelly turds, a block long, onto roads, causing major tailbacks around the country.

Likewise, he enjoyed spraying huge showers of urine, which cascaded down onto shops, houses and office blocks alike, soaking unlucky passersby.

He was too big to wear clothes and although only a child, his penis was now forty feet long which caused embarrassment and amusement in equal proportions as he strode around the country, causing minor earthquakes wherever he went.

"It's too risky to feed Oswald any more, sir," said the Head of the Army to the Prime Minister at a hastily-called emergency meeting. "Oswald sneezed and caused two transport choppers to crash, with the loss of twenty soldiers!"

"Hmm. Yes, Oswald is a problem all right. I'd like to use the nuclear option but it wouldn't be fair on the public who got vaporised or burned beyond recognition."

"Listen, sir, I've an idea that might just do the trick."

The Head of the Army continued and the Prime Minister began to smile.

And so, it was decided. A giant PA aboard a transplant plane was flown close to Oswald's head and a message was broadcast, giving him an ultimatum. Go to Africa or be attacked by the Royal Air Force!

So, the very next afternoon, Oswald began his trek to Africa. He waded across the English Channel in five minutes, causing a mini-tsunami along the coasts, and was soon striding down through France, Spain and some other unimportant countries.

He would snack on herds of sheep and cattle, popping them into his mouth and munching on them like crisps. For water, he carried an enormous pipe which he'd found on a building site, and which he would use to suck up water from lakes and ponds.

But this diet played havoc with Oswald's stomach and he had to squat several times to spray brown-orange diarrhoea over town and country alike. The people cursed Oswald, who, once a world-famous attraction, was now almost-universally hated.

"*Dieu merci, il est trop jeune pour se masturber!*" exclaimed the King of France as a thunderous rain of smelly yellow urine crashed down onto his palace and gardens.

Striding along at nearly five hundred miles an hour, it only took two days for Oswald to reach the Sahara, where he amused himself by kicking some pyramids around, much to the dismay of the locals who found *this* 'tourist' too big and strong to fleece.

So, Oswald was free to stamp around the Sahara Desert, which was nice and warm and, to him, like a giant sandbox. Here, he grew to be almost a mile high, taking the occasional foray south to snack on herds of impala, antelopes and zebras.

But Oswald was not happy. He missed his mother and father and his schoolfriends. Now he had no one. He was unable to talk or communicate with anyone. His voice was too loud and his size meant it was hard to approach people without squashing them. And it was very cold in the desert at night. He would lie, shivering and crying, keeping the natives of the Sahara awake. But they didn't really count, so to all intents and purposes, Oswald was isolated.

Then, after a week in the desert, the second part of the general's cunning plan came into play. Oswald was stomping around the desert, gazing out to Morocco in the North and thinking to drain a nearby oasis, being rather thirsty, when he spotted something moving – a tiny light, low down in the distance.

It came nearer and nearer and now Oswald heard the high-pitched scream of engines. He felt frightened. But after all, he was a mile high – invincible!

Then the tiny light began to rise above the desert, higher and higher, until it was level with his waist. Closer and closer it sped towards him, until, like an angry wasp, it buzzed at his chest. Oswald tried to swat it away but missed, then he felt a sharp pain. That was the last thing Oswald ever remembered. He was enveloped in a huge fireball as a five-megaton nuclear warhead exploded in his ribcage. The explosion was so enormous it could be seen from almost every country in Africa and the heat was so intense that Oswald was completely vaporised, along with some local tribesmen – 'unavoidable collateral damage.' So, there wasn't even the need to dispose of a hundred-ton corpse and a day of celebration was held all over the world.

Of course, some said that the action was cruel and wanted the Prime Minister to be prosecuted by the National Society for the Prevention of Cruelty to Children and there were violent demonstrations – as there always were about anything. But the Prime Minister would have none of it and went on television to give a speech about personally having saved the world from a terrible menace.

And as for the oh-so-wicked witch who had started it all. Well, whilst listening to the radio and the chaos her potion had wreaked, she cackled so much that she suffered a fatal heart attack. Her evil potions now stood on a shelf, in innocent-looking, anonymous glass bottles, waiting for the day when they would perhaps be found by an unsuspecting school child and, maybe, tasted once more.

The Ballad of Johnny Fang

There once was a lonely vampire,
Johnny Fang was the poor fellow's name.
All he wanted was a young lass to love him,
But, being dead, he was nobody's flame.

He'd wander at night through the graveyard,
By the light of the silvery moon.
Wondering how he could get him a gal,
Who, at the sight of his fangs, wouldn't swoon.

But Johnny had other desires,
For on blood he was destined to feast.
So, he headed off to the nurses' home,
There were women there, at least.

Now, the home lay down a lane called Ings,
A strange name, Johnny did think.
And he thought of winn-ings and end-ings and such,
And lust-ings for women in mink.

With his black cloak thrown all about him,
And wearing his tall black hat.
He thought he looked rather dashing,
Quite handsome, as a matter of fact.

Trying not to trip on the edge of his cloak,
He crept up the old marble stairs.
And into the little room at the end,
The abode of nurse Francine Pierres.

He gazed down with joy at her sleeping face,
Then down at her creamy white neck.
Lifting the cover, he looked further down,
Before giving her lips a quick peck.

Before she could let out a scream or a holler,
Johnny plunged in his fangs to the hilt.
He sucked up the tasty and tangy red blood,
While his hands did wander *sans* guilt.

Six months to the day, from the coffin he rose,
To a sight that gladdened his eyes.
For there in a shroud as pale as her skin,
Stood Nurse Pierres, as he'd oft fantasized.

"Oh, Johnny, you killed me," the young nurse did cry,
"But it's OK, I know you have needs.
And now I too fancy a nice drop of blood,
Let's stick together and see where it leads."

Well, Johnny thought all of his Christmases,
Had all come at once, and it showed.
Said Francine, "I've a nice coffin for two,
Down at the end of Vampire Road."

And so, Johnny got his sweet lover,
And Francine, she was over the moon.
But they'll be needing another coffin,
A little vampire is on the way soon.

The Boy in the Attic

"Word of advice, young lady."

Shannon Morris pulled a face. "What, Dad?"

"When Granddad tells you it's time for bed, it's time for bed, d'you understand?"

"Oh God, they go to bed so *early*. Granddad thinks half past nine is late!"

"Look, they're good enough to look after you for two weeks. Feed you, wash your clothes, drive you into town; the least you can do is show them some respect. D'you hear me, young lady. Hey …"

But she was already heading for her bedroom.

Shannon looked out through the window of her small, austere room onto rows of grimy terraced houses. How she hated the cramped bedroom, the smell of grandma's cabbage broth and her grandad's stinking pipe. And worst of all, no internet! All they had was a small black and white television in the front room. It couldn't even get Channel Four for heaven's sake! She felt tears of frustration. Her friends were all off on holiday. Spain, Majorca, Ibiza, even the more exotic destinations of Bermuda and Haiti, and here *she* was – stuck in bloody Blackburn!

But today was different. "Me and your grandad are going to Bingo tonight. We won't be back till late." said her grandma. "There's stewed cabbage on the stove and beef casserole in the oven."

Shannon brightened up. At least Grandma made good dumplings. And with them out of the way she could find a pop radio station and turn it up! "All right Gran, thank you. Have a nice time."

Shannon gave them half an hour then went under the stairs for the stepladder. She carried it upstairs, swearing loudly as it hit the banister, taking a lump out of it. She'd have to find some shoe polish to disguise it, at least till she'd gone home, though no doubt they'd complain to her parents. She climbed the ladder and pushed on the loft door, smelling mould and feeling a cold draft as it opened. She pulled herself up into the attic and, using her phone as a flashlight, looked around. She spotted an old Bakelite light switch on a rafter and, being careful to stand on a beam, reached out and flicked it. To her surprise, a dim yellow bulb covered in cobwebs sprang into life. She wondered how many months or years it had lain dormant.

She looked around at piles of packing cases and old suitcases. How boring! She'd hoped to find some interesting antiques or books or letters or something, not just bloody suitcases. She tried to open one but it was locked. She tried a couple more. On her third attempt, success. The lid of the case sprang open to reveal a couple of dozen shirts, all neatly folded and stinking of mothballs. They had the old 'grandad' style of collar, she observed. How appropriate. And boring! Next to them lay a bunch of desiccated flowers – roses and ferns and the like. A bride's posy she wondered? Perhaps Gran's? Hard to imagine her grandmother as a vivacious young woman!

On a cushion in the suitcase lay something more interesting, a small porcelain ornament. She held it up to the light, a round flask decorated with a red dragon, blue clouds and waves. Chinese she imagined. It must be worth a few quid. She slipped it into a pocket.

As she flicked the light off to go back down into the house, she noticed a glimmer of light from behind the chimney breast. She turned the light back on and made her way gingerly across the beams – she didn't want to go crashing through into her grandparent's bedroom. She manoeuvred her way around the chimney. To her surprise, there was a door and from beneath it, a chink of light. From behind the door came a strange sound, a mechanical sound she couldn't quite place. With her heart in her mouth she turned the knob and gasped as she stumbled into a well-lit room where a train was running around an expansive model railway layout. Oh God, a bloody boring train set! She turned around to go back when she heard a voice.

"Hello, who are you?"

A young man's voice. A youth of perhaps eighteen, a couple of years older than her, had appeared. He had a handsome face and curly blonde hair in an inverted 'v' shape that hung down to his shoulders. He gave a pearly-toothed smile and his blue eyes twinkled.

"Oh, er, I'm Shannon, actually."

He laughed' "Well, pleased to meet you, Shannon Actually! My name's Marty Brown. What are you doing here?"

Shannon found herself blushing, much to her surprise. "Oh, I'm staying with my grandparents next door. They'd gone to bingo and I ... I, er, I thought I'd take a look in the loft."

"Oh, you're not a nosy girl then!" Marty laughed. "Do you like model trains? I'm on holiday here for another two weeks. You could help me, er, reorganize the layout."

Shannon found herself short of breath. She felt dizzy, then Marty's arms around her, holding her steady.

'Are you OK?" he asked.

Shannon recovered but didn't pull away, enjoying the sensation of Marty's embrace. "Oh, sorry, I felt faint. I think it was ... er ... climbing that ladder."

"That's OK. Glad you're all right."

She put her arms around Marty. "Yeah, I'm fine and that'd be great, I mean I *love* model trains!"

Behind Locked Doors

"Look Mr Sissons, I'm sorry, that part of the graveyard's no longer used, on account of subsidence caused by badgers. Please see Fred, the sexton. He'll show you where new graves can be dug and sort out the availability, bearing in mind the ... ah ... timeframe." The Reverend Samuel Everson got up from the pew, feeling a certain trepidation and hoping the matter was now closed.

Edgar Sissons was a big man and leader of the local council. He wore a long black coat of thick woollen material and barred the reverend's way. "Look, Reverend, my Auntie Nellie's buried in that far corner, as you know. It's my desire that my sister Dolly be buried next to her, God rest her soul."

Samuel Everson felt his hands growing sweaty. "Look, Mr. Sissons, we all have the greatest respect for Dolly, but when all's said and done, she wasn't a regular churchgoer here, and as I say—"

"Listen, Reverend, it's my wish that Dolly be buried next to her kith and kin and from where I'm standing I see no good reason she can't be. The collapsing bit is more over to the other side."

The Reverend Everson felt emboldened. "I'm sorry, Mr. Sissons, I'm afraid it's out of my hands. Now, if you would kindly get out of the way please."

But Edgar Sissons didn't get out of the way. "Look, Reverend, you've put in a planning application for a new conservatory at the rectory. It's none of my business but it seems a pretty big one, huge you might even say. Look, if you could ... ah ... bend the rules a bit, then maybe the council will look more favourably on your application—"

"Cooee!"

The reverend was thankful to see Mavis Westerby, the postwoman, clutching a lengthy rectangular package. She made her way down the aisle to the two men. "Good morning, Reverend, good morning, Mr. Sissons. I've a package for the reverend to be signed for. By the way, did you hear about Fanny Sammons's trouble down at the hairdressers? Shocking it was!"

Before she could start on another of her interminable stories, Edgar Sissons made good his escape. "Good day, Reverend, I have to head over to the undertakers at Calthorpe now, please think over what we discussed. Good day, Miss Westerby."

The Reverend Samuel Everson breathed a sigh of relief. "Look, I have to go out presently, could you give me the short version please?"

Churches and cathedrals are replete with ancient, locked and bolted doors, full of mystery. St. Margaret's was no different and now The Reverend Everson felt a thrill of anticipation as, carrying the long parcel, he descended the stone steps to the crypt. Inside, he flicked on a dull orange lamp, passing stone shelves housing dusty coffins to a further, even more ancient doorway, hidden behind a black curtain. He unlocked the door with a large iron key from his cumbersome keyring, turned on another even dimmer light and proceeded down a cold, clammy tunnel that smelt of earth and mould. Somewhere above, how far he wasn't sure, but possibly too close for comfort, lay Auntie Nellie's bones.

Houses have their secrets too, and the Manor House was a notable example. A trapdoor opened in the cellar, displacing a carefully-positioned rug, and the reverend emerged, a little grubbier, with the box. Once in the house itself, he rang a small bell on a table. A woman in her fifties, blonde-haired, plump but well-proportioned, and clad in riding gear, appeared at the head of the stairs. She smiled and beckoned him up. "Edgar just phoned. He's going to Calthorpe, sorting out Dolly's funeral arrangements. We'll have a good hour or so."

The Reverend Samuel Everson climbed the stairs to the landing and proffered the parcel. "For you, Eunice." He felt breathless, though whether from the exertion he couldn't be sure.

"Don't worry about Dolly's grave, Sammy," said Eunice Sissons, pecking him on the cheek and proceeding to open the package with an ornate paper knife. "Edgar gets these silly ideas in his head. I'll talk him out of it, don't worry. And get him to approve your conservatory too. I have my methods."

"I'm sure you do," said the reverend.

"Oh, Sammy, how lovely, thank you so much!" Eunice brandished a shiny riding crop, cracking it loudly. "Come on, let's play horse and rider. Get on your hands and knees."

"What, right now?"

"Don't be silly," laughed Eunice, "get your clothes off first."

Martian Holiday

You could not reasonably say of Charles and Elizabeth Soulby that they had the characteristics of inveterate treasure hunters, but you could say that the curious force of money, the promise of it, had an unpredictable influence on their lives.

Charles was a fair young man with a tireless commercial imagination and an evangelical credence in the romance of business success, and although he held an obscure job with a bicycle manufacturer, this never seemed to him anything more than a point of departure.

"Y'know, Liz," said Charles one evening, "there's a guy at work, he's got a sure-fire idea to make one helluva lotta big-time dough!"

Elizabeth Soulby raised her eyebrows.

"Yeah, his name is Stanley, got an uncle by the name of Matthias Dale, a big shot in the aircraft business. Anyway, seems this Mr. Dale is offering shares in the first flight to Mars!"

Elizabeth Soulby raised her eyebrows even higher.

"Honestly sweetheart, this Dale guy knows what he's talking' about, got contacts in the air defence business."

Elizabeth squared her shoulders and put her hands on her hips. "Well, what the hell does this guy know that NASA doesn't know then!"

Charles sighed, "Simply this, he doesn't have a million and one regulations holding him back. *And* he has Fan Evans on his team."

"Who the hell is Fan Evans?"

"Only one of the top Mars experts on the planet!"

"Never heard of him."

Charles gave an exasperated look. "*Her*. Short for Fanny. Anyway, the fact you've never heard of her means jack squat."

"Charles!"

"Sorry, pardon my language, just look her up."

"So, who's paying for all this and how exactly do we cash in?"

"Well, look, Mr. Dale will sell us a franchise for a hundred dollars. We put adverts in shop windows, magazines and so on for people to invest a hundred bucks. For every thousand bucks we rake in, they'll do a raffle and one of the ten will go on to the final draw. And listen to this, we get ten percent commission, *and* we get a free raffle entry every ten thousand bucks. We can't lose!"

Elizabeth made a noise like a donkey farting. "Sounds like we start off losing a hundred bucks!" She poured herself a large measure of gin and added some ice cubes. "And how many will be in this final list then, for Christ's sake?"

Charles pushed a glass forward. "Fill me up, Liz, look, I dunno, just that the guy at work says some billionaire Saudi Arabian donor is going to increase the amount raised ten times!"

"Pfft. Probably won't even notice it, the amount those Arab sheik types are sitting on."

"Maybe he'll have to cut back on the handmaidens for a couple of weeks. Look, there's just one little snag."

Elizabeth snorted. "Oh, just the one?"

"Yeah, look, we've got to put our phone number. The idea is to weed out the weirdos."

Elizabeth clinked her glass against Charles's. "Well, here's to all the non-weirdos who want to spend their life on Mars, cheers!"

"Hi, I'm calling about your ad," said a woman's voice.

Charles couldn't believe his luck; he'd put the first card in a shop window just that afternoon. "Hi, so you wanna go to Mars then?"

"Well, not me, I'd like to send my husband."

"Well, that's OK, give me your address and I'll send you the papers. Send them back with a cheque for a hundred dollars and you'll be in the draw, as well as supporting a great adventure for mankind!"

"My name's Tabatha, Tabby for short, but look, if I send two hundred bucks do I get two shots at the raffle?"

Charles felt excited. Two hundred bucks! "Well, yes, but you'd have to send two separate cheques and they'd each go towards a separate thousand, if you see what I mean."

"Oh, sure, sure, I see. Look, what's the odds of my husband, Kenneth, well, I call him Kenny, Ken sometimes. What's the odds of him going to Mars then?"

Charles felt his hand sweaty on the phone handset. "Well, Tabatha—"

"You can call me Tabby."

"Ah, well, *Tabby*, it all depends how many are interested. It could be thou— er, quite a lot. But all the finances will be made public so you can get an idea. One in ten will go onto the final list, then four from that list will go on the first mission."

"Huh, it doesn't seem that likely Kenneth will go then!"

He heard Tabatha coughing at the end of the line. It sounded like she was a heavy smoker. "No, wait a minute. Don't forget there'll be a second mission and a third …."

"Yeah, but just how many lists are there gonna be, for Chrissakes?"

Almost exactly one year later, the Soulbys had signed up no fewer than five hundred would-be astronauts, netting a cool five thousand dollars commission, not to mention five raffle entries. Soon franchises were offered all over the world, where equally industrious salespeople had recruited tens of thousands of hopefuls and the Saudi Billionaire, much to his chagrin, had been required to increase oil production to keep his part of the bargain.

The rockets had been built and, thanks to Fanny Evans, plans had been made to set six astronauts down on the planet Mars forthwith, four raffle winners and two 'proper' astronauts.

"What's up, Liz?" Charles asked one morning, seeing Elizabeth's white face and shaking hands after she had just opened a long white envelope.

"Charlie, I don't believe it. You've been selected to go to Mars! My Charlie, a world-famous astronaut. I don't believe it!"

Charles snatched the letter out of his wife's hand and stared, disbelieving. "Good god, you're right, I'm going to Mars." He began to dance around the room. "We're all going on a Martian holiday …."

When he'd calmed down, he re-read the letter. "It says the priority of the first mission will be to search for life."

Elizabeth came over and placed one of his hands on her belly. "Charles, there's something I've been meaning to tell you. A new life is starting right here."

Charles stood electrified. "What, you mean …."

"Yes!"

"Then if I go to Mars, I won't see my son – or daughter, of course."

Elizabeth smiled. "I've just had an idea. There's nothing in the rules says you can't sell your ticket. It must be worth a fortune!"

Charles sighed. "Jesus, that must've been the shortest astronaut career in history!"

Dog Story

"God in a box, sis, gimme a break, I've been writing my balls off all morning!"

"Come on, you pwomissed. Anyway, how long does it take to write a five-hundred-word story for God's sake?"

"All morning – if it's for a magazine; it's gotta be just right."

"Well, what's it about?"

"It starts like this. 'You're not going to eat that thing raw, are you?' asked Prunella. Jack laughed. 'If it'll keep still long enough!'"

"Yuk, what's next?"

"You'll have to buy the magazine to find out!"

"I think I may not bother. Now come on, Uncle Doris is waiting." I sniggered at our private joke.

My brother, Paul, put his manuscript in a draw and pulled a pair of white trainers out from under the bed.

"Christ, haven't you heard of foot deodorant?"

"If you're that bothered go out and buy me some!"

"It's not me that has to suffer. It's poor Abigail. So many nice boys out there and she chooses you. I can't understand it!"

Paul grinned lasciviously. "Maybe I've got hidden talents."

"And there was me thinking she was a *nice* girl. Anyway, I'm not going out with you in those stinky things!"

Reluctantly, my brother pulled out a brand-new pair of smart brown leather lace-ups, an unenthusiastically-received Christmas present from mum.

The corridor was long, with pens on either side. Each pen had an upper and a lower door, both of glass. A record sheet within a holder gave information: *Name, age, sex* and *'fun things.'*

"I like this one," said Paul. A Pit Bull terrier, with a white muzzle and a black patch over one eye, saw us looking and got off his bed, barking excitedly. The sheet said *Tyson, 4 years, male, 'I like to chase squirrels!'*

"Can I see him?" Paul asked a lady in a red top and trousers, wearing a matching baseball cap with the logo: *The Ark Animal Rescue.*

"Sure, Tyson's a softie. Just the top door please."

Tyson jumped up, putting his paws over the top of the lower door and cocking his head to one side, making eyes at Paul.

"Hello, boy, good boy!" Paul stroked Tyson's head. Then the dog jumped down and ran to pick up a toy, a red bean bag. He jumped up again with the toy in his mouth.

"Ah, he wants me to throw it for him," laughed Paul, taking the bean bag from Tyson's mouth and hurling it across the pen. Tyson obliged by racing to pick it up, then returned to jump up again. Paul went to take the toy but this time Tyson kept his jaw clamped shut. "C'mon, boy, don't you want me to throw it for you?" They began a tug of war, the dog stubbornly refusing to let go of the toy.

Whilst Paul played with Tyson, I was taken with Honey, a brown Labrador Retriever. She sidled around her pen, barely looking up at me. I tapped on the glass. "Honey, hey, Honey!" She ignored me and returned to her bed. The sign said *Honey, 11 years, female, 'I like cuddles and leisurely walks.'* "What's up with Honey?" I asked the woman in red.

"No one wants a dog so old. I think she realises that; she's given up."

"Ah, what'll happen?"

"Well, if no one wants her after six months, she'll be euthanized."

"What, you mean … killed?"

"Uh huh." She looked away.

I felt a lump in my throat and wetness in my eyes.

"Stupid mutt!"

I turned to see Paul closing Tyson's door.

Uncle Doris appeared. "Hi Charlene, did you find one you liked?"

"Not yet," I said.

"Well, I've found a nice doggy. Come and see."

We followed him to the end of the pens. *There* was a Golden Retriever, a rusty red in colour. *Karma, 3 years, female, 'I like to play with children and swim!'* She jumped up, barking furiously.

The lady in red approached. "Would you like to walk her? You can take her out to the yard, I'll fetch a lead."

We all fell in love with her instantly. How on Earth could anyone have given her to an animal shelter? I wondered.

"Yes, please!" we all said in unison.

Back home, we high-fived each other, laughing, as Karma rushed into the house and up the stairs, barking enthusiastically, as if she'd always lived there. Dad appeared, smiling. "You found a dog, I gather!"

"She's a beautiful animal, Ted," said Uncle Doris, following us in.

Mum appeared from the lounge. "Everybody come through, there's something for Charlene."

We all traipsed into the lounge to find a huge cake in the shape of a cartoon bulldog, adorned with seventeen candles.

"Ah, Mum, thank you." I kissed her on both cheeks as the others started with a chorus of Happy Birthday.

At the last refrain we were startled by a loud barking. There was my new friend with a mangled white shoe at her feet.

"Hey, that's my trainer!" shouted Paul.

"That's Instant Karma for you," said Uncle Doris. Even Paul had to laugh.

The Bride

Weighed down with concerns, financial and otherwise, that to anyone dying of a horrible disease would no doubt seem trivial, I was surprised and, in a way, relieved to hear from my old friend Marmaduke Fortescue one evening.

"Stephen, you must come and meet my new bride … yes, that's right, I'm married!"

Well, you could have knocked me down with a feather, I'd never have put old 'Marmers' down as the marrying type. Not that I'd thought of him as queer, you understand, just that he was always off in some foreign country 'adventuring,' and the thought of him settling down had never seemed on the radar.

"I'll tell you no more right now," he said, "but are you free tomorrow evening? … You *are,* wonderful, come round at seven, you're in for a surprise!"

So, the following evening I'd driven down to Marmaduke's place out in the country, Fortescue Manor, where I was shown through to the salon by old Juggins, the butler. Marmaduke jumped up to shake my hand and I was surprised by his youthful appearance. He'd lost at least two stone since I'd last seen him, what, maybe a year earlier? And his grey hair was now a glossy black.

"Stephen, wonderful to see you, take a seat. What would you like to drink?"

Juggins brought me a bottle of lager whilst Marmaduke began to tell me about his new wife. "Now, I must warn you, Stephen, Asmarina is a little 'unusual,' but she's young, strong and healthy, and broody too!"

"What, you don't mean …."

"Yes, I've never mentioned it, perhaps, but a few little kiddies running around this old pile would liven it up a bit, don't you think?"

Just then, there came a distant thud, like a depth charge exploding, then a few seconds later, another, and then yet another. Marmaduke smiled. "I'm afraid Asmarina has some habits of her tribe, like doing her poo standing up."

"Her tribe!"

There now came a distant sound, reminiscent of a machine gun.

Marmaduke laughed, "Ah, my dear wife has a touch of diarrhoea, I'm afraid. It's adjusting to English food. I'm sure it'll pass."

I felt myself reddening. "Where is this lady from, then?"

"Ah, she's from the Dahlak archipelago."

"Where the hell is that?"

"Eritrea."

This felt like a game of twenty questions. "Where the hell is that?"

"It's at the bottom of the red sea, on the left, next to Djibouti."

"Ah, of course, good old Sheik Djibouti!"

Just then the door opened and Asmarina came in. Her face was brown with a flat nose and big round eyes. Her hair was black and frizzy in the style of the old 'fuzzy wuzzy' cartoons we had in comics when I was a kid. She wore grey socks, a dark blue skirt and a white top, like a girl's gym outfit. She wore no bra and her shirt was filled with what looked like two cherry-topped blancmanges.

"Hello, Mr. Stephen, I am enthralled to meet you."

"Er, likewise." I shook her sweaty hand, fervently hoping that her tribe had at least learned to wash their hands after 'poos.'

"Look, Mr. Stephen, I show you good trick."

Before I could stop her, Asmarina had taken out a box of matches and lay down on the carpet. Then she lifted her skirt, which left nothing to the imagination. Through thin violet briefs peeked a thick wodge of course black pubic hair, reminiscent of a Brillo pad. She lit a match and lifted her sizeable bottom up with brown muscle-bound thighs.

Marmaduke gave a knowing smile and wink. "Look out, Stephen!"

In a scene worthy of Aristophanes, Asmarina held the burning match close to her bottom and let out an enormous fart, producing a shooting flame that just missed my face.

There was the smell of burning nylon as Asmarina jumped up, laughing, to the applause of Marmaduke.

It looked like I was in for an interesting evening!

The Invisible Man

It was late in the afternoon when the bus stuttered to a halt outside the old hotel in the foothills. The town square was deserted, save for a cow in the shade of the once-imposing colonial buildings, swishing its tail by a water trough.

Inside, we sat on worn leather sofas in a huge vestibule, cooled by the blades of an enormous fan above. "*Buenos dias*," I heard a concierge say to our leader, West.

"What's your name?" a bespectacled woman asked me. Her hair was held back in a grey ponytail and her bare legs and calves were brown and pudgy. "Mine's Norma."

"Oh, it's Colin, pleased to meet you." Though I wasn't really.

"What do you do?"

"Oh, I'm a ... I'm a plumber."

"Oh, we'll know who to come to if we have any leaks in our room then!" She gave a laugh like a car backfiring. "This place is rather quaint, isn't it? Did you know there's been a drugs war around here? West was telling me on the way. Seven killed in this village last month, he said."

"Great. Actually, I thought it was further down the valley."

"It was right here. But the bad men are in jail, or dead, most of them anyway, apparently."

Just then I became aware of raised voices from the desk. After a while I heard West say, "All right, I'll tell him."

He came over and addressed the walking party. "Manuel, the concierge, tells me you can all collect your keys. There's a form to fill in, the usual passport number, date of birth, national insurance number etc."

We all groaned.

"But, Colin, I'm afraid there's a little problem. Could I speak to you in private, please?"

I looked out of the window, down onto the town square where a little brown boy in a yellow football shirt was poking the cow with a stick. In the room it was cool but outside in the square the flagstones were hot enough to fry a *tortilla*. I took a bottle of water and went to the bathroom to clean my teeth. "Don't drink the tap water," West had said, "and don't use it to clean your teeth either, unless you want dysentery."

I heeded West's advice, all the while fuming at the impossible choice I'd been given. Seems everyone else was with a spouse or partner or friend. Only West and myself were travelling on our own and he had a room in the concierge's house across the square. Due to an influx of mourners, the hotel was full and there was 'no room at the inn,' Manuel had been quite insistent on that. "*Lo siento señor, lo siento mucho*, er, I very sorry." He'd given me a choice, I could sleep in the cowshed "Is quiet there, *señor*, Bella she good cow, and hay is fresh." Or I could share my room with Carlos, a student staying a week for his uncle's funeral. The problem being that there was only one bed.

"Did you sleep well?" Norma asked me the following day, as we slogged up a muddy mountain track. It was the rainy season, apparently.

"I did, actually, thank you Norma. There was a drip in the shower, but fortunately I brought a monkey wrench and managed to fix it myself."

"Clever you." She gave a bright smile.

"Yes, and I tightened the tap washers too. One looked like it'd been fitted at least thirty years ago, but it was some weird size, not one I carry a spare of."

"Er, I met Carlos at breakfast, he seems a nice lad, very, er … animated, he speaks good English too. Tells me he's sharing your room."

"That's right, he'll be getting his head down right around now. Then he's up at four, he'll change the bedding and tidy the room and clear off by five. He's working overnight at a bar in the town for the week."

Norma nodded. "Ah, all's well then."

"Hm. Apart from him washing his socks and underpants in the sink and leaving them hanging over the bath. Oh, and he didn't bother to rinse the sink out afterwards either."

Just then there came a sound like a machine gun. Norma grabbed my arm with a vice-like grip. "Did you hear that?" Her face was white.

Well, I wasn't stone deaf. "Don't worry, it's probably just a drug gang fighting it out on the path up ahead."

"Don't worry everyone," bellowed West. "That was only firecrackers, they're having a little party at the next village. We've all been invited for a 'breakfast tequila.'"

A general cheer went up as West began to hand out party hats and masks.

I took a green hat and skull mask in disbelief.

He laughed. "It's a national holiday, the Day of the Dead!"

A Brush with Teeth

Known to my friends as a rather, dare-I-say, boring type – "Sammy doesn't even have a television, he reads *books*!" – and for someone who eschews festivities and hedonism in general, I surprise even myself with what I am about to reveal. How a staid bachelor-type, working in an admittedly mundane computing role, came to regularly indulge in an activity with a buxom young Thai that is, well, what some might call downright kinky. But I digress.

Well, there I was a mere six weeks ago, ambling along in my lunch break, when I passed a branch of Boots the Chemist. Rubbing a sore patch on my chin, I recalled I needed some new razor blades, the old fashioned-kind I favour, along with a genuine badger-hair brush and shaving soap. Being bamboozled by all the new-fangled shaving devices, I determined to waste no more time and headed towards the girl serving on the counter for directions to the plain blades I required.

The sales girl was occupied with a woman who reminded me of a circus clown, buying a stack of make-up. I marked time by looking at the electric razors, something alien to my upbringing. But my eye was caught by formidable black boxes containing electric toothbrushes. Just that very morning I'd noticed a yellow aspect to my teeth, years of smoking Woodbines in my youth I supposed, a habit inherited from my dear old dad. I reeled at the price of the things, anything from forty to a hundred guineas, daylight robbery, as dad was wont to say. Yes, I like to price things in guineas, it comes from a singular mental agility I possess. Odd, I know.

Anyway, at the top of the daylight robbery tree was the Titanium Shine, with its six settings: 'Clean, sensitive, gum clean, white, deep clean,' and the enticingly-named 'special clean.' Throwing caution to the wind, I took it to the desk, just as clown-lady left with enough bottles to make up the whole circus.

The girl looked me up and down, then smiled with dazzling white teeth. "I use one of these, sir, it's great. Your teeth will definitely thank you!" Then seeing me blushing, "Sorry, sir, I didn't mean to embarrass you."

"No, that's, er, that's quite alright." I paid for my package and hurried back to work to secrete it in my desk before the others returned from lunch. Only then did I realise I'd clean forgotten about the razor blades.

Well, that night I started a love affair. Just me and dear Titanium Shine. At first, anyway. It took three days to learn to keep my arm still and not move it up and down in a brushing motion, and to get used to the deep vibrations penetrating my teeth and jaw as it did its tooth-whitening work. After a couple of days, I began to read the manual in more depth. Seems there was a Bluetooth function to hook it up to my smartphone. Then I could see how often I'd cleaned my teeth, which setting I'd used, the length of time brushed and the estimated amount of plaque removed per brushing. And that information was sent to a 'dashboard' that opened in a browser window on my computer, allowing me to see my 'brushing history', 'cleaning profiles' and more. Amazing! What *will* they think of next? The only thing was that the damned toothbrush tended to spray toothpaste everywhere, so I took to cleaning my teeth in the nude, making sure the curtains were drawn of course.

Things developed. Not only did Titanium Shine give me all that, but there was also a forum where 'Titanium Shiners' could leave comments and ask for help about various tooth-brushing problems. And you could 'like' and 'friend' other tooth-brushing forum buddies, even 'unfriend' them if they got annoying. Well, one day I posted about a little problem I'd encountered. My gums would bleed after a couple of minutes of the 'special' and I had a helpful reply from a Thai lady, Suchada. After a few days of tooth-brushing chit-chat she began to private message me, firstly about the type of toothpaste she preferred, then about her husband and how he was unfaithful to her.

Well, that wasn't what I'd bargained for at all but then she began to send me photos of herself and I had to admit she was a 'looker,' even in mid-brush, and I always did favour oriental women. Soon she was suggesting a 'meet up' to discuss our experiences of the different settings. She said the 'special' 'did something to her,' but she'd have to tell me in person.

In for a penny, and a week later Suchada called round. Turned out she lived in the same town, conveniently. Well, she was one attractive woman, perhaps forty, but pretty damned sexy I had to admit. Well, after some tea and biscuits and chit chat, seated at my little 'Fortnum and Mason's table,' she said "Sammy, my teeth feel, how you say, a *leetle* sugar-coated. Where is bathroom please?" Then, blow me, she pulled out her Titanium Shine, winked, and headed off, beckoning to me as she reached the door.

So, now we have a little ritual. We stand cheek to cheek with our Titanium Shines, then the music starts. I like "Saturday Night Fever," she likes Chic. There's much hilarity and a great 'vibe' between us as we 'do the bump' on the same settings. I'm plucking up the courage to ask if we could clean each other's teeth, but perhaps that's going too far, don't you think? Well, Suchada just messaged me to say she likes my idea of cleaning teeth in the nude. She says the Titanium Shine *is* a little messy, particularly on the 'special,' and would I mind if we tried it together? Well, it couldn't do any harm, I suppose. Could it?

Memory Lane

It could have been right out of one of my own sitcom scripts. I received a telephone call late one evening from an old lady, Miss Jean Sycamore, if you please. She was most insistent that I undertake some detective work for her. I tried to tell her that I was a TV comedy scriptwriter and not a detective, but she said she'd heard I'd written some episodes for *Detecting the Detectives,* a CID spoof, and being that I lived locally, she was prepared to pay me a handsome price to find a lost object.

So, the following morning I called round to her rambling country estate, Enderby Manor, where I was shown in by a crusty old butler who could have been acting in *Toad of Toad Hall.* "Madam, a Mr. Frederick Rossiter to see you," he announced in a wheezing voice to a rake of a woman with a wild frizz of white hair.

She got up from a sofa and peered at me. "Mr. Rossiter? No, I don't think I know such a fellow."

"Look, Miss Sycamore, you phoned me last night. You told me you wanted me to find something for you. Something valuable I assume."

The old woman looked perplexed. "Did I? Did I really?" She stood staring into space for what seemed an age, then her frail body shook all over, as if she'd been given an electric shock, and she suddenly smiled at me. "Mr. Rossiter, thank you so much for coming. That'll be all Porterhouse. I do apologize, Mr. er, ... I'm afraid my memory isn't what it once was. Now, please take a seat. Porterhouse will get you a drink. Oh, sorry, I sent him away, didn't I?"

I sat down. "Look it's OK, I don't need a drink. How may I help?"

"Well, you see, I'm looking for a mirror."

Maybe I should have had that drink? "Well, they sell them all over the place. You could try Boots, you know."

She made a gesture as if swatting a fly. "Oh, don't be a rascal, I mean *my* mirror, a special mirror I've had since I was a girl. And that was a long time ago I may tell you!"

Well, seems this mirror was stolen in a burglary some months earlier, some jewelry and furs too. But Miss Sycamore shrugged her shoulders. "They can be replaced. And they were insured too." She gave a falsetto giggle. "For a lot more than they were worth!"

But it was the mirror she particularly wanted back, a small hand mirror in the shape of a butterfly and with a minor defect in the handle, she told me. She offered me a thousand pounds, a reward I could sorely use, the TV writing lark having been sketchy at best of late. To look efficient, I took a list of the other stuff taken, a pretty impressive haul, for reference. In fact, a copy of one given to the police who had failed to recover any of the stolen property so far.

I made enquiries with an acquaintance of mine, a gypsy fellow by the name of Cullum who had his ear to the ground, and his one good eye on the constant lookout for anything that had 'fallen off the back of a lorry.' His other eye had been lost to a gamekeeper's shotgun pellets.

Time passed and Cullum had nothing to report, and I'd almost given up on Miss Sycamore's precious mirror when one weekend I noticed a sale of bric-a-brac at the local village hall and for no real reason decided to take a look.

I was pleased to find a good book stall where a wealth of paperbacks and the odd hardback were just twenty-five pence each or four for a pound. Well, that's what the sign said. I found a few titles in the Penguin Play series, where a number of the plays were comedies from the sixties, always good to refer back to the 'old masters' I think, when comedies were actually funny and made you laugh.

I recognized old Oswald Farthing and his enormous wife, Bessie, who latched onto me, the latter insisting on describing at great length her method of making lemon curd. Just as I'd almost reached breaking point, I spotted something that quite took my breath away. There on the table, right behind her huge bottom, was a box of odds and ends, and blow me, right at the back, a mirror in the shape of a butterfly.

"Fred, are you OK?" Bessie was asking, but I only had eyes for the mirror. Picking it up, I noticed the characteristic bullet hole in the handle Jean Sycamore had described. I paid the very reasonable asking sum, excused myself from Bessie's curd-making instructions, and made a bee line for Enderby Manor.

Porterhouse eyed me curiously and showed no sign of recognition as I explained who I was and why I was there. He ushered me into the lounge where Miss Sycamore sat on a sofa, staring into space. She looked right through me, as if I wasn't there, then her eye fell on the handle of the mirror which was sticking out of my jacket pocket. A strange transformation came over her as I pulled it out. She jumped up and seemed to glow all over. "Oh, Mr. er ... how wonderful of you to find my lovely mirror. I had this as a child, you know. I am so grateful to you. Look, Porterhouse will bring you some tea and biscuits, and I will show you photographs of when I was a little girl, holding this very mirror!"

Seeing her excitement, I felt loath to mention the reward but, well, needs must. "Er, Miss Sycamore, would it be possible to have the reward in cash, please?"

"Ah, the reward ... yes ... um." She rummaged around in a box for a minute. "Ah, here it is!" She held up a photograph of a young woman dressed as a cowboy. "I don't remember saying anything about a reward, dear. Look, this is me when I was eighteen. I performed in a rodeo show in South Dakota, can you believe!" She began to hum an old show tune as she looked in the mirror, holding the photograph against the glass and gazing at it lovingly.

Two hours later, I made my escape, somewhat shell-shocked by the arduous trip down memory lane. But there was one consolation. The lady who sold me the mirror had remembered where she'd bought it. From a 'woman who looked like a gypsy.' She'd had two young urchins in tow and a husband lurking in the background. A husband with one eye. Which would explain why Cullum had come up with nothing regarding the robbery. And, in fact, the insurance company were offering a hefty reward for information leading to the recovery of Miss Sycamore's stolen jewelry and furs. I decided I didn't owe Cullum any favours, so it looked like celebrations were on the horizon after all. And as for Miss Sycamore, well, she would serve nicely as the inspiration for 'Calamity Jean,' a character in my latest sitcom.

As Safe as S*it

On the transatlantic flight, the valuable cargo was in a briefcase in a sealed blue bag, wedged between two security guards. Sleep and toilet breaks were taken in turns, so the precious cargo was not left alone for a second. Well, that was the theory ….

"I'm heading for the bathroom," said George Holland.

"Huh?" said Alfred Marwood.

"The little boy's room, y'know."

"What?"

"The restroom!"

Marwood laughed, "Oh, you mean the bog!"

"You Brits!" Holland said as he got off his seat in a hurry and disappeared.

What the hell was in this briefcase? wondered Marwood. All he knew was that it had been a big … well, *huge* operation. Whatever this thing was had been protected by gun-toting security men on its way to JFK airport. They'd been told to guard it with their lives until they landed at Heathrow airport, England, where they would be met by armed guards.

Alfred Marwood looked around. Nothing unusual, passengers snoozing, or eyes glued to some crummy movie. He examined the seal on the bag. A simple heat seal. He took out a small device and ran it along the seal, opening it with ease. It would be child's play to reseal it. Nothing to worry about.

Next, he tested the buttons on the briefcase. No movement. He felt in his pocket for something no one knew he possessed, a kind of skeleton key, privy only to the higher echelon of security guards. He tried it and, to his surprise, the lid sprang open.

"Excuse me, sir, would you like anything to drink?"

Holland's heart skipped a beat as he looked up into the eyes of a blue-eyed, blond-haired, low-cleavaged air hostess. "No, no, I'm fine, thank you."

The young woman shrugged, disinterested, as she moved to the next row.

Holland lifted the forbidden lid and saw a black plastic bag with a zipper. He recognized the tag on the zipper, a radio tag, a tag that would send an alarm to ... someone ... if pulled. Hmm. Better forget about it. He closed the briefcase and was just ready to click the locks back into position when he remembered something. He opened the lid again.

"Find anything interesting?" It was Holland, back from emptying his bladder, however you wanted to express it.

Marwood jumped. "Hi, George, look, just wondering what the hell it is we're guarding."

"None of our business," said Holland.

"But, like, wouldn't you be interested, seeing as there was all that commotion, armed guards and all the rest of it?"

Holland sighed. "Well, I guess it's a diamond or something. They wouldn't tell me, just said it was worth millions, and to keep schtum about it."

"Millions!" said Marwood. "Well, wouldn't you be interested to just take a peek?" He opened the briefcase again and held a squat black device against the black plastic bag. "EMF shield," he said cryptically, then he drew the zipper back to reveal a red box. Once more the skeleton key proved it was worth every penny of its hefty price tag.

"The moment of truth," said Holland as Alfred Marwood lifted the lid of the red box to gaze at the treasure.

"Blimey," exclaimed Marwood, "I'm well underwhelmed!"

In the box was what appeared to be two pieces of glass, with a tiny piece of pink paper with ink marks on it sandwiched between them.

"What is that. It looks a bit like a stamp. Is this some kind of piss take?" asked Marwood

"Look," said Holland, "no crummy little bit of paper is worth an armed guard, there's got to be something else in there, hidden somewhere." He looked around the plane. Everyone was engrossed with the movie where a woman was taking her clothes off. He began to rifle through the briefcase, box, and bag.

"Ladies and Gentlemen, please take your seats," came an announcement, "we will shortly be landing at Heathrow airport."

"Look out," said Marwood, "you've put greasy fingerprints all over that glass. Didn't you wash your hands?"

Holland looked embarrassed, "Look, I'll just give it a quick rinse in the bathroom."

Moments later a breathless Holland came back from the toilet to his seat. "Phew. Nice and clean. Let's seal everything up."

Marwood stared in disbelief. "Where's that little piece of pink paper?"

The blonde stewardess was coming out of the toilet. "Did someone leave this in the sink?" she announced, holding up a tiny soggy pink thing.

Sheepishly, Holland went to retrieve it.

The plane engines began to roar as they hit the runway and the plane began to slow down. Holland was feeling some concern. The small piece of pink paper hadn't looked so good when they'd put it back between the glass and back in the red box, black liner, briefcase, and blue bag and sealed them all up again. Though the glass was nice and clean.

"Oh … my …god," said Marwood, noticing a huge poster behind an armed escort waiting outside the terminal as the plane finished taxiing.

Holland craned his neck, reading out loud. "Never has so much been spent on so little. London welcomes the one cent British Guiana Crimson stamp. At seven million dollars per square inch, the most valuable man-made product ever made!"

"Bog, restroom, khazi, shithouse, I don't care what you call it," exclaimed Marwood, "I need it and I need it now!"

A Question of Semantics

Lighted from above by three bright spotlights, a dartboard was mounted on the yellowing paint of a wall in The Golden Calf. It stood in a corner, housed in a cabinet with blackboards for scoring on the inner side of each cabinet door.

It was only Thomas Scaman's second visit to The Golden Calf, having moved to the village of Little Muchly with his wife, Judith, just two weeks earlier. Their first visit had been at lunchtime and the pub had been full of jovial families with their kiddies.

Tonight, he'd fancied a pint, and leaving Judith to her writing he'd headed down the lane to the pub, expecting to be met with a friendly greeting and to make new pals over a game of 'arrows.' As a former league player, he expected to be met with, well, a kind of hero's welcome, he told himself. Instead, he opened the door onto an empty, sparsely furnished, and equally sparsely populated, bar.

A couple of old men were playing dominos, not troubling to look up from their game as he entered. The only other occupant was a youngish lad with a gormless face, sitting picking his nose and grinning like he'd just won the lottery.

"Good evening," said Thomas. There came the click of dominos and a high-pitched giggle from the young man, who Thomas now noted had bulging crossed-eyes, red cheeks, and large wet lips. Thomas wondered if the boy was recovering from a bad beating, but then decided it was his natural face.

"Can I help you?" A man stood behind the bar, long grey sideburns growing on his sagging jowls and his stomach sticking out in a prominent beer belly. Above the bar was a faded photograph. A man with a grim wheel-like face and a long silver wig glared through the dirty glass. Underneath was the legend, 'Theophilus Leake, 1762-1849, Founder of Shadford's Brewery.'

Thomas hesitated, eying the door regretfully. Then he noticed a beer brewed by Shadford's. "Er, a pint of Persian Silk, please."

The barman yanked on a handle, pumping a mass of foam into a glass. "It'll settle in a moment, it's a bit lively."

Just then a couple of young men came in. They stripped off heavy coats to show muscled arms covered in tattoos. One of them had a large anchor tattooed on his wrist. He slapped a set of darts down on the bar. "Pint of Hebrew Hoodoo please, Bill, when you've finished serving this ... gentleman." They both laughed.

"Do you play darts then?" Thomas ventured.

"No, that's why I carry a set of darts around with me," said anchor-tattoo man. He made a noise like a fart.

"Oh, er, sorry, um, would you, er, like a game?"

"What, maybe later mate, hey, Bill, you got any pork scratchings?"

Thomas took his beer over to the dartboard and took a few self-conscious throws, hearing the men chuckling at the bar.

"Fancy a game then, mate?" it was anchor-tattoo man.

"Oh, yes, that'd be good," said Thomas.

"Fred'll chalk," said the man, "501 straight start, you throw first."

Fred stood at the side of a blackboard with a piece of chalk in his hand, ready to record the scores.

"Oh, OK, thanks." Thomas took aim at the treble twenty, the highest score on the board. His first dart just grazed it, his other two landed in the adjacent sectors, five and one, for a score of 26, known to dart players as 'bed and breakfast.' He felt his face flush as anchor-tattoo man hurled his first dart straight into the middle of the treble twenty followed by two close by, for a score of a hundred.

"Tony's brilliant," said Fred, revealing anchor-tattoo man's name, after the former had emerged victorious five games in a row. "He can put three darts in the middle of a polo mint."

There came a high-pitched giggle from the young lad.

Thomas felt the Persian Silk going to his head. "Never!"

"Yeah, he can." It was the barman.

"I'll bet you, then," said Tony, "Do you drive?"

"What, yes."

"Well, I'll have one go at putting three darts in the centre of a polo mint. I do it, I take your car. I don't do it, well, Bill here will give you and your mates free drinks for as long as you're alive. Ain't that right, Bill?"

The barman assented with a grunt.

The young man, whose name turned out to be Percy, stood grinning like a Cheshire Cat, holding a small round mint with a hole in it, in front of the dartboard. Tony took aim. Thomas stood, wondering how he could lose, surely this guy wasn't *that* accurate? Then, to his incredulity, Tony walked up to the board and poked his three darts into the centre of the mint. He turned, "Car keys please."

Thomas stood, stunned, "What are you on about, you never threw them!"

The bar was deadly silent. Tony held his hand out. "Don't you understand the meaning of the word 'put'?"

"Hold on a minute, you've got to be joking." Thomas felt as if his body had just been placed in a deep freeze.

"No joke," said Tony, "hand over them keys, or …" He and Fred slipped on large silver knuckle-dusters.

To his horror, Thomas noticed that Bill had disappeared, as had the domino players. Only Percy remained, his mouth wide open and his giggling stalled for once.

Then the door opened and in came a police constable. He looked around the bar in astonishment. "Come on, Tony, you at it again? Haven't you won enough cars already!"

The Price of Silver

Saunders & Swindell – said the sign. Well, the last bit wasn't far off the mark, thought Geoffrey Green. Below the sign, three spheres hung from a bar – the international sign of the pawnbroker.

Green gazed into the window. Several guitars hung on the right-hand side, likely the result of an aversion to practice, coupled with the need for beer money. Before him were rows of TVs and laptop computers, and to the left, in a heavily-barred section, row upon row of rings, broaches and pendants. Then there were several *Victorinox* penknives for travellers. He wondered if they still had a blade for removing stones from horses' hooves

The prices were generally quite affordable, bargains even. Reflecting the prices paid, he mused.

On the top shelf were antiques and bric-a-brac, and in the centre, an oil painting of a young woman in a white summer dress, standing in a garden amongst a rainbow of blooms. The price tag said £500. Thank God it hadn't been sold! He pushed the door open and went up to the counter.

A small, wiry man appeared. His face was blotchy, and his eyes small and bloodshot. A thin grey stubble covered his cheeks and chin, and beneath a pointed nose, crooked yellow teeth formed something that might have been a smile. "Can I help you, sir?"

He reminded Green of a hungry ferret. "Yes, I sold you a picture, the girl amongst the flowers, it's in the window."

"Ah, yes, I remember you, sir. Unfortunately, the option to buy it back expired yesterday." The yellow teeth disappeared behind compressed thin lips.

"Yes, I know, I couldn't get here yesterday." Green fought off the memory of alcohol poisoning.

"Well, I'll tell you what, sir. I'll knock ten percent off. You can buy it back for £450, how does that sound?"

"Thanks, that'd be good."

"Cash only."

"Ah ... I haven't got the cash, but I've got this ...." Green pulled a heavy silver plate out of a holdall and placed it on the counter.

The ferret wore a badge that said Robert. He stared long and hard, then he picked the plate up, examining it closely, his narrow, disagreeable face inscrutable. Around the edge of the plate were embossed heads of notable Roman and Greek gods and dignitaries. He ran a nicotine-stained finger over a bust of Diogenes. "Just a minute, sir." He disappeared with the plate.

Green stood, looking around at the goods on display, quite oblivious to them. Nervously, he looked at his watch. Twenty minutes till closing. Twenty minutes to get the picture back before his uncle would return from holiday the following day to find it missing. Then all hell would break loose.

After a few minutes, the ferret returned with the silver plate and a magnifying glass. He seemed jaunty, self-important. "Where did you get this, sir?"

Green decided to tell the truth. "Actually, my brother and me were digging some foundations the other day. We found it buried a couple of feet down."

"Er, was there anything else with it, sir?"

Green looked at his watch. Why wouldn't this horrible little man simply make him an offer? "Look, does any of this matter? I want some cash so I can get my picture back!"

"Calm down, sir. Look, I'll tell you a little story." The ferret took a seat behind the counter and jabbed at his gum with a toothpick. Green could see blood on it.

"Well, it so happens that any gold or silver found buried in our fair land belongs, not to the finder, but to the Crown. It's 'treasure trove,' it is, and must be declared immediately to the police. This is Roman, this is. Solid Roman silver! And it's valuable, you could likely buy a hundred of your pictures with this!"

Green felt his stomach sinking to the ground. "Well, no one has to know, do they?"

"Ah, that's where you're wrong, sir. We pawnbrokers have principles, you know. This must go straight to the police. But the *good* news is that the finder will be paid its full value ... in time." He raised his eyebrows. "Plus that of any other pieces found with it."

"Er, well, in that case, could I get the picture back against the *promise* of my ... er, reward?" Green asked, hardly able to believe his luck.

The ferret smiled a yellow smile. "You didn't hear me properly, sir, the *finder* gets the full value, and you told me it was you *and* your brother, but you can't *both* have found it. It was one or the other!" He laughed. "Whoever it was is going to be a rich man ... eventually. You can sort it out between you! Either way, if you want the picture, you need to pay now – cash only."

"What? I'll have it back then!" Green reached over and snatched the plate from the ferret's hands.

The door opened behind him and the ferret's face turned from a look of total astonishment to one of triumph.

Green felt a hand on his shoulder. "Going anywhere with that, sir?" asked the policeman.

Gender Concerns

Feeling a little apprehensive, I went into the hotel, passing a smiling receptionist, then through to the bar and restaurant area. Smartly-dressed family groups ate at tables or sat in a more casual area with sofas, easy chairs, and leafy potted trees, drinking coffee or sipping wine. Quiet jazz music played in the background. For some odd reason I suddenly had an image of a group of skinheads bursting in, all braces, high Dr. Martens and shaven skulls. Up-ending tables and hurling them around, smashing glass and porcelain alike. People screaming as jabbing fists and thudding boots left a trail of broken and bloodied bodies.

Fortunately, nothing like that occurred, and the sound of a gentle, tinkling jazz piano solo was all there was to be heard.

At one table sat a young woman, conspicuously alone, looking at her phone. That must be my blind date, I thought, Jules. As I grew closer, she looked up, put her phone down and smiled. "Hello, are you Vincent?"

"Yes, nice to meet you. Can I get you a drink?"

"I've ordered a coffee. I gave them my card. Just ask the waiter for whatever you like, he'll put it on the card."

"Oh, that's kind of you, thank you." I took my jacket off, put it on the back of the chair and sat down.

"So, Sarah's told me a lot about you," she said.

"Oh." Sarah was my big sister. I wasn't sure what there was to tell exactly, and I couldn't imagine it being favourable, the way I knew she'd tell it anyway.

"Me and Sarah were close at Uni – that was a while ago! We shared a room on the farm, did she tell you?"

"No … no, I didn't know that."

She began to reminisce about their days at agricultural college. I looked at her and wondered ….

She had short brown hair and an oval face, quite pink, healthy looking, with no make-up. She wore a green tunic top and new 'designer' jeans with smart brown leather boots. Her chest seemed quite flat – two small lumps. Her teeth were white and even and her voice was mid-range in pitch.

As she chatted, and I attempted to make intelligent noises, I realised there wasn't much to mark her out as specifically feminine. Her skin looked to be smooth, though, no sign of a beard.

Sarah had said Jules was 'special,' and there was something strange in the way she'd said it, a hint of a smile playing on the corner of her lips.

The waiter brought her coffee and I ordered a pint of lager. "Sarah said you work in healthcare," I remarked.

"Well, my path has meandered a bit. I went into yoga and meditation classes, then counselling, now I'm a gender-assignment advisor." She smiled, noticing my bewilderment. "I still work for the NHS, though." She sipped some coffee, leaving a brown rim above her upper lip.

"Oh, that sounds, er … different." I wondered if I should say something about the stain on her face.

As if reading my thoughts, she extracted a tissue and wiped her mouth. "Yes, things have got a bit complicated nowadays. There's gender binary and cisnormativity." She laughed. "Male and female, if you like. Then there's what some call genderqueer. Those are people you may call bigender, trigender or pangender." She stopped talking and looked down, sipping her coffee as the waiter deposited my lager before me, in a tall elegant glass. He put her card on the table, together with a receipt. "Thank you, madam."

"So, what exactly do you do then?" I asked.

"Well, we have to match the perceived sexual identity with the actual, er, attributes desired." Noticing my blank look, she said, "In other words, whether they want a cock and balls, vagina or tits."

A portly lady in red at a nearby table looked around. Jules stared at her and she hurriedly looked away, carving into her coq-au-vin, face flushing.

Embarrassed, I took a gulp of lager, feeling the alcohol rushing to my brain. I realised I hadn't eaten for hours.

"You see, we have the medical technology available now to offer a full range of options. Some of it will be covered by the NHS, for instance if a boy wants to be a girl and they can prove it's a deep-seated desire and last the assessment course. But others, well, they just want a bit of fun, but of course they have to pay for it!"

"Oh." I'd planned to talk about my work as a car dealer but it would no doubt seem deadly dull compared to the 'characters' she came up against.

She hesitated. "I'm sorry, I need to pop to the loo. Can you look after my handbag please?"

"Yes, no problem."

I watched her walk briskly away and noticed a direct motion, a lack of sway. The toilets were through a side door at the far end of the restaurant area, and once she'd passed through it, on impulse I quickly followed her, oblivious to the regular family chit-chat going on around me. I reached the door to the toilets and, opening it, saw the men's toilet door swinging shut.

Not daring to go in, I took a chance and opened the ladies' loo door, ready to apologise effusively. However, all the cubicle doors were open, no one there!

I hastily retreated and made my way back to the table. An elderly couple sat in silence nearby, nursing glasses of red wine and staring blankly at each other.

"Could you tell the young lady that I had to go please, keep an eye on her bag?" I asked.

They looked up, surprised, then appeared pleased to have something useful to do. "Of course, er, should we say why?" said the lady.

"Oh ... thank you ... er, yes, gender concerns!"

I quickly made my way to the exit, leaving them looking at each other in bewilderment.

Goodbye Bernie, Hello Samantha

"Say it ain't so, Joe, please say it ain't so," Samantha Muir sang whilst hanging out leather belts in the Ladies' Accessories department of Jacksons. *"That's not what I wanna hear, Joe. Ain't I got a right to know?"* She hesitated. Why was she singing that? Her mind flashed back to a scene when she was nine years old, her little brother Joe coming to her with blood pouring from his nose. An older boy, Terry, had punched him in the face at the bus stop after school.

"Excuse me, young lady, are you serving or dreaming?"

Samantha looked up to see an old lady, slim with white hair and dressed in a purple cloak and black hat, though it was a fine spring day outside. "Sorry, can I help you madam?"

"Indeed, you can, my dear, I'd like a silk scarf, something beautiful – if you have such a thing."

Five minutes later, the old lady was twirling around in front of a mirror with a grey chiffon scarf hiding her wrinkled neck. It featured butterflies and peacocks in a contrasting purple. To Samantha's surprise the woman burst into song. *"I could have danced all night, I could have danced all night,"* whilst waltzing around the floor.

Samantha couldn't help but join in. *"And still have asked for more. I could have spread my wings—"*

In harmony they sang, *"And done a thousand things ...."*

"Thank you, Miss Muir, that will be all," came the loud croak of Ms. Steel, the manageress. "Kindly get back behind the till and serve this good lady. Now, I have to attend to a crisis in the shoe department." She exited the accessories department, huffing and puffing.

"Oh, I don't much care for her!" exclaimed the woman.

Samantha bit her lip.

"By the way, my name is Millicent Lawson." The old lady offered her hand. "You may have heard of me."

Samantha blushed, "No, madam, I'm sorry, I haven't."

Millicent began to tap dance. *"Smile, though your heart is aching, smile—"*

"Even though it's breaking," joined in Samantha, warming to the woman's eccentricity.

"When there are clouds in the sky, you'll get by."

Millicent stopped in mid-tap. "Just a minute, dear, how old are you, if you don't mind me asking."

Samantha blushed, "That's OK, I'm twenty-four."

Millicent approached Samantha and gazed at her with wide hazel eyes. "You've a good memory for songs, my dear, before your time too!"

Samantha hesitated. "Yes, well, to tell you the truth, Madam, er, Millicent, once I hear a song, I never forget it."

"What never?"

"No, never."

The old lady burst into song once more. *"What never ... hardly everrr. Hardly ever swears a big, big D,"* singing the lines from *HMS Pinafore*. Then she stopped abruptly and handed Samantha a card. "My son, Andrew, is in the music publishing business, give him a call. *Then give three cheers, and one cheer more—"*

Samantha threw her arms wide. *"For the well-bred Captain of the Pinafore!"*

Ms. Steel's croaking voice was icy. "Miss Muir, will you *please* stop larking around and serve this customer at the till!"

Two weeks later, having thought of every reason *not* to phone Millicent's son in the meantime, Samantha finally gave in to curiosity and plucked up the courage, scarcely imaging why he would want to speak to her.

"Good afternoon, Lawson's Music Publishers, can I help you?"

"Er, well I'm not sure. Mrs. Lawson, er, Millicent, said to phone Andrew, her son. My name's S-Sam ... Samantha Smith."

A moment later, Andrew came on the line. "Hi, Samantha, I've been waiting for you to call. What took you so long? And may I call you Sam?"

To Samantha's surprise, Andrew was friendly and chatty, then, "Is it OK if I test out your claim?" he asked.

She suddenly felt confident. She trusted her memory completely. "Er, sure."

Twenty minutes later she had reeled off the complete lyrics to nine of the ten songs Andrew proposed. Songs from shows, the charts, even old black and white films. The other one she was certain she had never heard.

Andrew laughed. "That's incredible! Look, we could really use some new song writing talent right now. With your amazing memory of melodies and lyrics, surely you could put together an, er, ... amalgam of bits from here and there, disguising them a bit of course, to make a ... well, a chart-topping hit?"

Was this really happening? thought Samantha. "Er, I don't know."

"Well, have a go, send me a recorded clip in a week or so. It doesn't have to be anything fancy, just the basic chords and melody. Millicent tells me you have a good voice, and do you play the piano or guitar?"

"I can play the piano a bit, but I don't have one."

"Right, give me your address and I'll have one sent round. One you can plug headphones into so as not to annoy the neighbours!"

Samantha laughed, thinking of cantankerous old Mr. Belcher. "Yeah, that might be useful!"

One year later to the day, Samantha sat crashing out chords on a walnut-cased baby grand. She didn't need headphones anymore and Mr. Belcher, Jacksons Department Store, and the croaking Ms. Steel were history. She gazed out of the windows onto a lawn where a pigeon was preening itself on a sundial. She could hardly believe her luck. She had to keep telling herself that, yes, it was all real.

She'd needed a few days to get the idea of creating something new, as opposed to just singing other people's songs, but by taking a couple of bars from here and an influence from there, she'd begun to come up with some snappy tunes. And the lyrics were even easier, she could write them in her sleep, and often did.

It had taken her half a dozen songs to fine-tune her talent then, *bingo*, she'd hit pay dirt with her next song, the funky *Devil on the Mountain*. It had been taken by Adele and now it pounded out in every bar in the world. Of course, Joe Public wasn't particularly interested in who wrote the song, so she had a degree of anonymity and that suited her just fine. The money was what mattered and it just kept rolling in. She looked around the room to where three gold discs hung in a row. Room for a few more!

The phone rang. She looked at the number and smiled. Robbie Williams. Well, let him wait. First, she had to return a call from Elton. Goodbye Bernie, Hello Samantha?

Appendix – Word Count of Stories

No.	Title	No. of Words
1	Contact	900
2	Dinner with the Colonel	900
3	The Listening	700
4	Danny and the Dolly Bird	1100
5	Tranquil Beginnings	900
6	Never Lovelier	850
7	The Magic Roundabout	500
8	When the Fat Man Croaks	900
9	All Apologies (A Writer's A-Z)	2200
10	Animal Magic	800
11	Pie in the Sky	1100
12	What's in a Name?	600
13	Shelly in the Jungle	650
14	Something to Do With the Sea	750
15	Wounded Walking	900
16	Tastes Like Hippopotamus to Me	800
17	Here's Looking at Your Kid	650
18	Stone the Crows	800
19	The Name is Grey	550
20	The Old Fuse Trick	950
21	There Was None Bolder	1100
22	Letters from Reuben	700
23	Free Money	650
24	*In Memoriam*	800
25	Postcard from Hispaniola	150
26	Just One Little Crumb	1700

No.	Title	No. of Words
27	The Ballad of Johnny Fang	369
28	The Boy in The Attic	900
29	Behind Locked Doors	700
30	Martian Holiday	1100
31	Dog Story	850
32	The Bride	650
33	The Invisible Man	800
34	A Brush with Teeth	900
35	Memory Lane	1200
36	As Safe as S*it	900
37	A Question of Semantics	950
38	The Price of Silver	850
39	Gender Concerns	1000
40	Goodbye Bernie, Hello Samantha	1100

By Simon J. Wood:

To Cut a Short Story Short: 111 Little Stories

A young magician in a pub opens his hands to release a cloud of tropical butterflies; a female bookseller is forced to attend a dance in drag to atone for a misdemeanor; a lonely man searches for a mysterious woman on a cruise; four school friends experience terror on a caravan holiday, and a macabre stranger wanders the streets at midnight, stealing dreams.

Ranging from just 100 up to 4000 words, these and 106 other memorable little stories are found in this eclectic and tantalizing collection by Simon J. Wood, an exciting new voice in the Flash Fiction genre.

256 pp. June 2017

ISBN-10: 152134311X, ISBN-13: 978-1521343111

eBook: ASIN: B071ZQGBR4

Bound in Morocco

A short story of intrigue, set in Morocco.

Marcus Slater decides to forgo the cold, wet, wintry weather of England to join a walking party in the sunny climes of Morocco. There, against a backdrop of the curious, ancient towns of southern Morocco he meets the enigmatic Sylvia and finds himself embroiled in a game he cannot possibly afford to lose.

42 pp. May 2017

ISBN-10: 978-1521324660, ISBN-13: 978-1521324660

eBook: ASIN: B071ZBK245

To Cut a Short Story Short, vol. II: 88 Little Stories

A husband, trying to rekindle his marriage in a lonely seaside village, meets a strange young woman from his forgotten past; a man taking a garden gnome to a museum gets an unwelcome surprise; a lonely widow encounters an enigmatic character from an embryonic pop group; a group of scientists make a horrific discovery at a big cat conservation centre; and a baby hare comes of age with a momentous idea.

Continuing in the spirit of To Cut a Short Story Short [volume one] these and 83 other stories, varying from 100 to 5000 words, are found in this eclectic and scintillating collection of 'flash fiction' by Simon J. Wood.

314 pp. December 2018

ISBN-10: 1719970092, ISBN-13: 978-1719970099
eBook: ASIN: B07L66S2N2

N.B. The above three titles are also available as audiobooks, narrated by Angus Freathy. Obtainable from Amazon, Audible, and iTunes.

The Window Crack'd and Other Stories: 40 Little Tales of Horror and the Supranatural

A man accepts a bet to spend the night in a haunted library; a young couple swim in an abandoned quarry, with unexpected consequences; four teenage girls decide to put the legend of Bloody Mary to the test; a man investigates a bookmark found in a book on demonology; and a young girl is convinced that someone or something is trapped in an old wardrobe.

These and thirty-five other unsettling stories by Simon J. Wood, a master of the 'flash fiction' format, will have you by turns smiling and sleeping with the lights on!

160 pp. December 2021

ISBN: 9798776204326

To be published December 2021

Flash Friction - To Cut a Short Story Short, vol. III: 72 Little Stories

240 pp. ISBN: 9798777357861

Don't lay me in some gloomy churchyard shaded by a wall,
Where the dust of ancient bones has spread a dryness over all,
Lay me in some leafy loam where, sheltered from the cold,
Little seeds investigate, and tender leaves unfold
There, kindly and affectionately plant a native tree
To grow resplendent before God and hold some part of me.
The roots will not disturb me as they wend their peaceful way
To build the fine and bountiful from closure and decay,
To seek their small requirements so that when their work is done
I'll be tall and standing strongly in the beauty of the sun.

WOODLAND BURIAL – PAM AYRES

Printed in Great Britain
by Amazon